Tales from
China's Classic
Essential Readings

中国蒙学经典
故事丛书

Tales from the Three Character Classic

《三字经》故事

郁 辉 *Yu Hui* ◎著

[美]艾梅霞 *Martha Avery* ◎译

CHINA INTERCONTINENTAL PRESS

五洲传播出版社

前言

　　中国古代重视对儿童和青少年的教育，产生了多种流传很广的启蒙读物，以使学生加强修养，增长智慧。《三字经》《百家姓》《千字文》和《幼学琼林》就是这些蒙学读物中的佼佼者，它们的主要功能是使学生认识汉字，并对他们进行文化和品德教育。

　　这些蒙学读物内容通俗易懂，形式简单，读起来很像歌谣，非常适合读者朗读和背诵。对很多中国人来说，这些读物是对他们一生影响最大的书籍，他们通过这些读物认识汉字，了解中国的历史、地理、社会等多方面的知识，并受到品德教育。直到今天，中国人仍然喜爱和重视这些蒙学读物。

　　上面提到的四本书中，《千字文》产生最早，是南北朝时梁朝人编写的，4个字一句，共250句，1000个字，所以称为"千字文"。

　　《三字经》产生于宋代，并经过后人的修改。它每句3个字，所以叫"三字经"。全书总共约500句，其中讲的许多观念和道理，对中国人影响深远。《三字经》已经被联合国教科文组织选入儿童

道德修养的必读书目，译成多国文字，在全世界范围内发行。

《百家姓》也产生于宋代，是有关中国人姓氏的启蒙读物，采用4个字一句的歌谣形式，共计568字，介绍了504个中国人的姓氏。

《幼学琼林》在这四本书里产生最晚，是明朝人编写的。它内容极为丰富，几乎是一部小型的自然和社会百科全书，所以有人说"读了《幼学》走天下"。

这些书中蕴藏着丰厚的中华民族历史文化传统，尤其是其中提到的那些隽永、生动的故事，令读者印象深刻。"中国蒙学经典故事"丛书从上述四本书中精选出一些在中国广泛流传的故事，以简短而生动有趣的文字讲述出来，通过它们，向全世界广大的读者介绍中华民族的历史文化知识和思想、道德观念。书中的故事分成若干现代人容易理解的类型，并配以幽默生动的漫画。

这套丛书不仅适合儿童和青少年，也适合广大对中国文化感兴趣、初步接触中国历史文化的读者。

Preface

The ancient China long ago has stressed on the child and youth education. Many primer readings spreading far and beyond came into focus, thus strengthening the cause of child upbringing and brightness. *The Three Character Classic, the Hundreds Surnames, the Thousand Character Classic, and the Children's Knowledge Treasury* are the best examples of such primer readings. Their main goal is to enable the child to learn characters and educate them about culture and morality.

The readings are easy to understand, and simple to read and recite as they resemble songs. They influenced the lives of many Chinese. They learned Chinese, as well as gaining knowledge on Chinese history, geography, and society. They are well-educated on morality too. Till today, Chinese still love and stress these readings.

Of the above-mentioned four books, *the Thousand Character Classic* came out earliest. It was compiled by a man of the Liang Dynasty. With four characters in each sentence, there are 250 sentences and 1,000 characters in the book. Due to this reason, the book is titled *the Thousand Character Classic*.

The Three Character Classic came out during the Song Dynasty times and was modified later. As it has three characters in each sentence, the book is titled the Three Character Classic. It comprises about 500 sentences. Many

ideas and truths in it have profound impact on the Chinese people. UNESCO incorporated the book into a list of compulsory books dedicated for the child moral education. It was translated into many languages and circulated globally.

The Hundreds Surnames came out during the Song Dynasty times. It is a primer reading related to the Chinese surnames. With a total of 568 characters and in the form of songs with four characters in each sentence, it introduced 504 Chinese surnames in all.

The Children's Knowledge Treasury came out the latest. The people of Ming Dynasty compiled this book. With rich contents, it became a mini-encyclopeadia of natural and social sciences. It owns the reputation of "Making you knowledgeable enough after reading *the Children's Knowledge Treasury*".

We can see profound historical and cultural traditions clearly in these books - especially those vivid and meaningful tales greatly impress the readers. *Tales from China's Classic Essential Readings* has selected tales spreading far and beyond in China from the above four books and tells them in short, lively and interesting truths. Readers, around the world, can learn the historical and cultural knowledge of the Chinese nation, ideology and morality through them. The tales are divided into categories to be easily understood by modern people, with the support of humorous and vivid cartoons.

The books are not only suitable for children and youth, but also for readers with interest in Chinese culture. They can experience the contact with Chinese history and culture.

Contents
目录

历史故事
Historical Tales

Studying Encouraging Tales
劝学故事

孟母择邻

原文：

xī mèng mǔ　　 zé lín chǔ

昔 孟 母 ， 择 邻 处 ，

zǐ bù xué　　 duàn jī zhù

子 不 学 ， 断 机 杼 。

故事：

　　孟子（前372—前289）是中国战国时期（前475—前221）一位伟大的思想家、教育家，他名叫孟轲（kē），孟子是人们对他的尊称。他继承并发扬了孔子的思想，被认为是仅次于孔子的儒家宗师。孟子能取得这么大的成就，与母亲从小重视对他的教育是分不开的。

　　孟子的故乡在现在山东省的邹城，祖上是贵族。在他很小的时候，父亲就去世了，家境不好。孟母做织布等工作辛苦地养家，但她并不因此而放松对儿子的教育，希望他将来能成为一个有思想、有学问的人。

　　起初，他们居住的地方靠近一块墓地，不时有人来这里举行葬礼。年幼的孟子和邻居的小朋友们跑去观看。举行葬礼的人走了，他们就模仿那些下葬、跪拜、伤心痛哭等动作，觉得很好玩。孟母看到这种情况，觉得这种环境不适合孩子求学上进，就宁愿多花一些钱，搬到一条热闹的街道上去住。

搬到新家没多久，孟母又发现了新的问题。原来，周围邻居大都是做生意的，离他们家不远处就有一家卖肉的店铺。孟子跟邻居那些孩子们很快熟悉了，经常跟他们一起到肉店去看热闹，然后就玩起做生意的游戏来：有人假扮卖肉的商人，有人假扮买肉的顾客，讨价还价，玩得十分高兴。当时的中国社会，人们认为经商是一种低贱的职业，商人在

社会上不受尊重。孟母不想让儿子将来成为一个商人，于是她决定再次搬家。

搬到哪里去呢？孟母经过慎重考虑，决定把家搬到学校的附近。

当时的学校设在王宫附近，是贵族子弟受教育的地方。孟子听到学校里孩子们的读书声，也跟着读。另外，每个月的农历初一、十五这两天，官员们都要到这里举行祭祀仪式，大家按照规定互相行礼，显得优雅庄重。孟子看在眼里，记在心上，回家去把这些礼节学给母亲看。孟母看到儿子新学习的这些东西，终于放心了，欣慰地说："这才是适合我们住的地方呀！"于是他们就在这里定居下来。母亲还把孟子送去上学，这一来她的负担更重了。

有一天孟子去上学，没到放学时间，就早早跑回家了。孟母正忙着织布，见他回来，就问："学习怎么样了？"孟子支支吾吾地答："还行吧。"孟母知道他是因为贪玩而逃学了，很生气，但并没有直接指责他，而是拿起剪刀，把刚刚织好的布剪断了。孟子很不安，问母亲为什么这样做，孟母说："读书求学就像织布一样，必须不断地积累，才能有所成就。剪断的布还能有什么用呢？你荒废学业，后果也是这样。"孟子十分后悔，向母亲承认了错误。此后，他严格要求自己，勤奋好学，终于成为有名望的学者。

Mencius' Mother Chooses Neighbors

Mencius was one of China's greatest philosophers and educators. He lived from 372 to 289 BCE, during the Warring States Period (475–221 BCE) in Chinese history. Although he was respectfully addressed as Meng-zi in Chinese, his name was Meng Ke. Considered second only to Confucius as a master of the Ru school of philosophy, known as "Confucianism" in English, Mencius both taught and further developed Confucian ideas. His accomplishments would not have been possible without the all-abiding importance that his mother placed on his education.

Mencius' homeland was a place called "Zou" in what is now the province of Shandong. His father died when he was young and the family circumstances were difficult. His mother worked as a weaver and at other jobs to support the family. Despite all, she did not let go of her belief in the importance of education; she hoped that one day Mencius would become an educated man with his own ideas.

At the very beginning, the family lived near a graveyard. People would frequently come by to conduct funeral rites and the young Mencius and his friends in the neighborhood would run over to watch.

After the mourners had left, the boys would mimic what had taken place, the lowering of the coffin, the kneeling and praying, the wailing and mourning. They thought this was all good fun. Mencius' mother looked upon this as a poor environment for getting a proper education. She decided she would rather spend a little money and move to a place

that was on a regular street and that had a livelier atmosphere.

Not long after moving to a new home, Mencius' mother discovered a new problem. All of the neighbors in the new place were involved in trade, and the family of one small friend had a shop that dealt in meat. After watching the comings and goings at the meat shop, Mencius and his friends would play at doing business, one the buyer, one the seller, haggling over prices, having a great time. At that time in China, tradesmen were regarded as being engaged in the lowest and most humble occupation. People in business were accorded no respect. Mencius' mother was now afraid that her son would become a businessman, so she determined to move again.

This time, after long consideration, she decided to move the family to a location that was near a school.

Schools were generally situated near the homes of the well to do at the time, near "princely homes." They were set up for the purpose of educating the sons of aristocrats. From where he lived, Mencius could hear the sounds of the children's voices, reciting their lessons. He was soon mimicking them, reciting the lessons as well. Moreover, on the First Day and the Fifteenth Day of every lunar month, officials would gather at the school to conduct rituals. As per the proper way of doing things, everyone would perform rites that seemed wonderfully elegant and sophisticated and grand. Mencius observed these things minutely,

and would then run home to perform the same rites and rituals in front of his mother. Seeing how well her son was learning these new things, Mencius' mother was relieved to have found the right place to live in the end. The family continued to live on in this place, and eventually Mencius' mother sent her son formally to the school, even though this added to the burdens she already had to bear.

One day, Mencius went off to school but returned early, before it was time for the lessons to be over. Mencius' mother was weaving away when she saw him come in. "How are the studies?" she asked. Mencius equivocated and just said, "Fine." Mencius' mother knew that he was playing hooky since he wanted to go outside and have fun. Upset, she did not scold him directly. Instead, she took up a pair of scissors and cut through the fabric that she was in the process of weaving. Mencius was appalled. He asked his mother what she was doing. "Studying is just like weaving a piece of cloth," she said. "It has to be a continuous accumulation of woven threads, or else it comes to nothing. What use is a piece of fabric that has been cut in two? If you waste the opportunity to study, the results will be just as useless." Mencius was mortified and promptly acknowledged his mistake to his mother. From that time onwards, he was strict with himself about his studies. In the end, he became the renowned scholar that we all know about as a result.

孔子的老师

原文：

xī zhòng ní
昔 仲 尼 ，

shī xiàng tuó
师 项 橐 ，

gǔ shèng xián
古 圣 贤 ，

shàng qín xué
尚 勤 学 。

故事：

儒家的创始人孔子（前551—前479），生活在距今两千多年的春秋时期（前770—前476）。孔子是人们对他的尊称，他本来的名字是孔丘，又叫孔仲尼，出生于现在的山东省曲阜（qū fù）市。作为一位伟大的教育家，孔子教出了许多优秀的学生。他知识渊博，但仍然勤奋好学，谁掌握他所不知道的知识，他就将谁当成老师。他不但向很多名人请教，甚至还将一个七岁的小孩当成老师呢！

孔子和学生们周游列国，一天，他们乘着马车走在路上，车突然停了下来。原来路中间有几个小孩，正用土和石子在地上建一座小小的"城"。见马车过来，其他孩子都躲

开了，但还有一个孩子不动。负责驾车的学生大声对这个孩子说："快给马车让路！"孩子却理直气壮地反问："只听说马车遇到城池要绕过去，哪听说过城池要给马车让路呢？"

孔子从车上下来，看看是怎么回事。这孩子活泼可爱，孔子一问，才知道他叫项橐（tuó），只有七岁。孔子很耐心地问："我们急着赶路，你为什么要阻挡我们的车子呢？"

项橐说："我并不知道你们要过来，我只是在这里修筑城罢了。现在城快修好了，你们不能从城上走过去，必须绕着走。"孔子问："你修建城做什么用呢？"项橐回答："如果有敌人侵犯我的家园，我就用它来抵御敌军的车马。"当时中国分成很多诸侯国，他们之间经常发生矛盾和战争。孔子听了，不禁（jīn）惊讶，觉得项橐很早熟。

这时，孔子的学生们拿了一些赌输赢的玩具给其他孩子，他们都高高兴兴地到路边玩去了，项橐却仍然待在"城"这儿不动。孔子好奇地问："难道你不想跟他们一起游戏吗？"项橐回答："这种游戏没有什么意义。如果人们迷恋这种游戏，玩得忘了时间，还可能影响工作、学习和其他重要的事情呢！小孩子就更不应该参加这种游戏，何况修建城的事情还没做完。"说着，就低头继续认真地修"城"。

孔子发现项橐与众不同，想进一步考考他，就说："我问你几个问题，如果回答不出来，就要给我们让路！"项橐答应了，于是孔子提出一些有趣的问题，没想到项橐对答如流，而且有些答案很巧妙。当项橐知道眼前这位老师就是见多识广的孔子时，说：

"我也问你几个问题，如果答不出来，就要拜我为师。"孔子也答应了，于是项橐反问了几个问题，比如鹅、鸭为什么能浮在水面上，大雁的鸣叫声为什么那么响亮，松树和柏树为什么冬天也不掉叶子。当时的人们对这些问题还没有科学的解释，孔子按自己的理解尽量解答，但项橐对他的答案并不满意，提出了疑问。孔子诚恳地说："我确实不知道这些问题的准确答案，你有资格做我的老师。"他恭恭敬敬地向项橐行礼致敬，项橐也恭敬地还了礼。

项橐继续认真地修"城"。孔子上车，让学生调转马车，绕开那座小"城"而去。他对学生们感慨说："这样的年轻人真是令人敬畏！我更加相信这样的道理了：三个人同行，其中必定有人有资格做我的老师。"

The Teacher of Confucius

The founder of the "Ru" school of philosophy was a man respectfully known as "Kong-zi" in Chinese, or Confucius in English. He lived from 551 to 479 BCE. He lived during the Spring and Autumn period of Chinese history (770 to 476 BCE), more than two thousand years ago. Kong-zi's original name was Kong Qiu, and he was also known as Kong Zhongni. He was born in the city of Qufu in Shandong Province. As a great educator, Confucius taught a number of outstanding students. Broadly versed in many subjects, he himself nevertheless continued to take an active delight in learning and he was delighted when someone knew things that he did not know. He was glad to consider other people his own "teacher." He not only asked for enlightenment on various subjects from famous people, but is also known to have regarded a seven-year-old boy as his tutor.

Confucius and his disciples or students travelled far and wide, riding in a cart pulled by horses. One day, the cart suddenly stopped for, in the middle of the road, some children had built a small walled city, a kind of castle. Seeing that a cart was coming, one boy stood his ground while the rest of the children scattered. The driver of the cart

shouted out to the boy to make way. The child stood even more resolutely firm, and shouted back, "I've never heard of a castle having to give way to a horse-cart! I've only heard of horse-carts going around a castle!"

Confucius descended from the cart to see what was going on. He saw that the little boy was quite alert and likeable, so he asked his name and learned that it was Xiang Tuo and that he was seven years old. Confucius then asked, in a very gentle manner, "We are trying to get along this road. Why is it you are blocking the way?" The boy replied, "I had no idea you would be coming by. I've just been working hard building this fortress. I've almost got it done. You can't go over it, you'll have to go around." Confucius asked, "What are you building it for?" Xiang Tuo responded, "If enemies were to invade our home, I would use it to hold back their horse-carts." At the time, China was divided into many principalities that were frequently at war with one another. Hearing this response, Confucius could not help but be impressed by the precocious young child.

At this point, the others in Confucius' party gave some small toys to the other lads, who were delighted to accept them and were soon playing against one another in the road. Xiang Tuo did not budge, however. He continued to stand guard over his fortifications. Amazed, Confucius asked if he didn't want to play with the others. "That kind

of thing doesn't interest me," said Xiang Tuo. "If you play around, you might lose track of the time and that might affect your work, your study, other important things! Children should not participate in those games, especially when they still haven't finished building a fortress." At that, he put his head down and again applied himself to his castle.

Confucius then knew that Xiang Tuo was different. But he decided to test him further. He said, "I'll ask you a few questions, and if you

can't answer, then you have to let me pass!" Xiang Tuo agreed. To Confucius' surprise, he not only answered well but some of his answers were marvelously ingenious. Once Xiang Tuo learned that the gentleman before him was the renowned Confucius, he said, "Now I will ask you some questions, and if you can't answer, then you must regard me as your teacher." Confucius also agreed. Xiang Tuo proceeded to ask him things like, how is it that ducks and geese can float on top of the water, why is the call of the great swan so very piercing and clear, why don't pine trees and cork trees lose their leaves in the winter. These questions had no scientific answer at that time, so Confucius answered them according to his own way of understanding things and Xiang Tuo was dissatisfied with the results. Confucius confessed quite openly that he had no idea how to answer these things accurately, and he said to Xiang Tuo, "You are certainly qualified to be my teacher." He bowed before Xiang Tuo in a gesture of respect, and at the same time Xiang Tuo bowed to Confucius.

Xiang Tuo then continued his careful building of the castle. Confucius climbed back up on the cart and instructed his disciples to detour around the "castle" and proceed. As they drove off, the Master said to his disciples, "Such a person is truly admirable. I am even more convinced of the principle that, 'Among three people walking along, one will surely be qualified to be my teacher.'"

赵普读《论语》

原文：

zhào zhōng lìng   dú lǔ lún
赵 中 令，   读 鲁 论，

bǐ jì shì   xué qiě qín
彼 既 仕，   学 且 勤。

故事：

　　赵中令指的是北宋（960—1127）初期的赵普，他曾经帮助宋太祖、宋太宗兄弟建立宋朝，立下很大功劳。宋朝建立后，他先后三次担任宰相，是这两位皇帝最信赖的大臣。

　　赵普年轻时候主要从事具体的行政工作，这方面的经验很丰富，但他读书不多，没有多少学问。宋朝建立以后，宋太祖兄弟注重文化教育，希望国家由一批有学问的人来治理。两位皇帝自己带头读了很多书。开始的时候，赵普有点不以为然，不愿读书。然而随着国家各项事业逐步发展，他发现自己的经验越来越不够用。宋太祖有时向他请教一些以前朝代的制度，他都回答不上来。

　　中国的皇帝即位以后，会给自己起一个含有称赞、祝愿之意的年号，这种年号通常不能与以前的帝王取过的年号重复。宋太祖取了一个年号"乾德"，赵普称赞说这个年号很好，而且没有人用过。后来宋太祖占领四川，得到一面年代已久的铜镜，惊讶地发现上面竟然刻着"乾德"年间制造的字样。这是怎么回事呢？站在旁边的赵普什么也说不出来。宋太祖找来另外两个学识渊博的大臣询问，才知道以前四川地方有

一个君主叫王衍，他曾经使用过"乾德"这个年号。这样，宋太祖的年号就与王衍的重复了，不得不另外选择一个。宋太祖不高兴地对赵普说："看来担任宰相的还应该是读书人啊！你应该多读一些书。"赵普感到很尴尬。

经过这件事之后，赵普暗下决心要多读书，以弥补学识方面的欠缺。这时他已经四十多岁了，而且每天要处理繁重的政事，但他仍然抽出时间来读书。他的桌子上堆满了各种书籍，回到家里，就关起门窗专心阅读。他读书很勤奋，拿起书就放不下，很多书的内容都牢牢记在心里。慢慢地，他的学识就丰富起来。尤其是朝廷遇到什么大事、需要制定什么重要政策时，他更是勤于查书，所提出的意见都有根据。等到他给宋太宗当宰相时，所写的文件已能熟练地引用古代典籍来说明自己的观点。

赵普活了七十多岁。他去世之后，家人打开他的书箱，里面放着一些他经常阅读的书，其中一部是记录孔子及其弟子言行的《论语》。在当时，这部书是儿童都读得懂的简单读物，赵普为什么还要经常读它呢？那是因为书中包含了从自我修养到治理国家的一套道理，赵普从中得到很多启发。

宋太宗知道赵普去世的消息后，感到失去了一位重要的大臣和老友。他亲自写了一篇纪念文章，其中特别提到，赵普晚年刻苦读书，变得很有学问，很多饱读诗书的老学者都无法跟他相比。

Zhao Pu Reads *the Analects*

Zhao Pu is also known as Zhao Zhongling. This man lived during the Northern Song Dynasty (960–1127), which he helped establish for the two brothers called Song Taizu and Song Taizong. After the dynasty was founded, he served as its Prime Minister three times and was the man both emperors most relied upon and trusted.

As a young man, Zhao Pu served in administrative capacities and had extensive experience in running governmental affairs, but his knowledge of academic matters, his book-learning, was minimal. Once the dynasty was founded, the two Song emperors' brothers began to emphasize the role of education and to hope that a group of scholars could be nurtured who would help govern the land. The two brothers themselves took the lead in reading many books. At the beginning, Zhao Pu felt this was somewhat beneath him and he did not follow suit. As the country prospered and things became more complex, however, he soon found that his own experience was increasingly inadequate. Song Taizu would sometimes ask him how a previous dynasty had handled this or that problem, what their systems were, and he would not be able to answer.

When Chinese emperors assume the throne, they give themselves a reign name that is generally in praise of the reign and that bodes for its prosperity. This reign name should not duplicate any that has come before. Song Taizu adopted the reign name of "Qian De," and Zhao Pu praised the choice, saying that it was excellent and moreover had not been used by anyone before. Later, Song Taizu invaded and occupied Sichuan, and there he was given an ancient copper mirror that

had etched on its back the reign name, "Qian De." Zhao Pu, standing beside him when this was discovered, could find nothing to say. When Song Taizu asked two other official-scholars with extensive book-learning about reign names, they soon were able to inform him that a King named Wang Yan had taken his reign name in Sichuan. Song Taizu's reign name duplicated Wang Yan's, and therefore had to be rejected and a new name had to be found. Song Taizu is believed to have said to Zhao Pu, "It looks as though a Prime Minister should be a man of letters as well! You should read a few more books." Zhao Pu took the advice to heart.

He applied himself to reading books in order to make up for his deficiencies on the learning front. At this time, he was already over forty years old, plus he had to manage highly complex governmental affairs every day. Still, he found time to read. His desk would be piled high with books, and once he got home at night he would close the doors and windows to any distractions and begin to read. He was highly conscientious and would not put a book down until he had finished it. His memory could recall all the contents of any given book. His knowledge gradually increased and also became more useful. When the court met up with some difficulty or major policy issue, he could consult various books and have some backing for his recommendation. By the time he became Prime Minister for Song Taizong, he was

already adept at quoting from the classics in his written arguments as a way to buttress and explain clearly his own point of view.

Zhao Pu lived to be over seventy years old. When he died, his family opened up the case that held his books and discovered in it many of the books that he had read most often. Among them was a volume of *the Analects*, that recorded the words of Confucius and his disciples. At the time, this book was read by children and was regarded as quite a simple work, easily understood, so his family wondered why he clearly had consulted it so often. It was because the book contained an entire coherent set of concepts that went from self-cultivation all the way to administering matters of state. Zhao Pu greatly benefitted from it.

When Song Taizong learned the news that Zhao Pu had died, he felt that he had lost not just a key minister but an old friend. He personally wrote a memorial for him, in which he specifically mentioned how Zhao Pu had enjoyed reading later in life and had become such a great scholar that many erudite men were unable to match him.

路温舒用蒲草抄书

原文：

pī pú biān   xiāo zhú jiǎn
披蒲编，削竹简，

bǐ wú shū   qiě zhī miǎn
彼无书，且知勉。

故事：

中国西汉时期（公元前206—公元25），河北巨鹿地方有个人叫路温舒，出生在一个看门人家里。看到其他孩子去上学，他也很想去，但家里太穷了，父亲只好让他去牧羊。

路温舒决心自学，他白天放羊，晚上就去请老师教他识字。渐渐地，他认识的字越来越多，能够读书了。他想看书，可是当时纸张还没有发明出来，书都是抄写在竹简或者丝绸上的，只有少数地位高、又有钱的人家才拥有藏书。通过老师介绍，路温舒到这种人家去借书看。他起早贪黑地读，恨不得把这些书都背下来。但借

来的书总是要还的，他想，如果能把书抄下来该多好！可是家里根本买不起抄写书的材料，怎么办呢？

有一天，路温舒到河边放羊。河边长着很多蒲草，

他灵机一动：蒲草的叶子宽宽的、长长的，不是可以代替抄书用的竹简吗？他割了许多蒲草，将它们切成跟竹简一样长短，放在太阳下晾晒。等蒲草干了以后，他就在叶子上工整地抄写，最后把这些写满字的蒲叶用线编连在一起。这样，一册"蒲草书"就完成了。看着这亲手制作的书，路温舒非常高兴，他终于拥有自己的书了！

从此路温舒学习更加勤奋。他到处借书、抄书，不断制作"蒲草书"。白天去放羊时，他随身带一本书，羊吃草或休息的时候，他就随时阅读。时间一年年过去，路温舒抄写的"蒲草书"装满了屋子，他也变成了一个有学问的青年。

西汉时期，政府特别注重法律条文，路温舒所读的书有不少是关于法律的，他决心凭借所学的知识去谋生。他先到本县的监狱去，做了一个低级别的管理员，继续学习法律知识。后来，凡是县里面有什么法律方面的疑问，向他咨询，总能得到满意的答案。县的上一级是郡，郡的长官发现他的才干后，将他提拔到郡里去。他又学习了历史书《春秋》等许多典籍，成为既有学问又精通法律业务的官员。他办事认真，廉洁自律，名声越来越大。

几年以后，皇帝也听说了路温舒的名声，就将他提

拔到中央政府。路温舒从自己的任职经历中，深切感受到当时的法律制度有很多问题。他上书汉宣帝，指出当时法律制度很严苛，很多人被处死或斩断了手、脚等部位；官吏严刑拷打囚犯，这种情况下，什么样的供词拿不到呢？他请求改革法律制度，废除一些严刑酷法。这些主张和建议得到汉宣帝赞同，并予以实施，使人民免受了很多痛苦。路温舒后来担任了最高司法长官，但他一直没有忘记从那些自制的"蒲草书"中获得的东西。

Lu Wenshu Writes on Cattail Leaves

Lu Wenshu was born into the family of a man who served as a guard at the gates of a particular household. He lived in a place called Julu in Hebei Province, at the time of the Western Han Dynasty (206 BCE–25 AD). As he watched other children head off to school, Lu Wenshu ached to join them, but could not, since his family was poor. Instead, his father sent him off to tend sheep.

Lu Wenshu determined that he would learn on his own. In the daytime, he tended sheep; at night he would seek out teachers to teach him how to write a few words. Gradually, the number of words that he could write increased and he found that he was able to read. He very much wanted to read, but at that time paper had not yet been invented. So-called "books" were generally copied onto bamboo strips or onto silk fabric. Only a very few people of high status were able to get hold of these, and only the very wealthy actually had what could be called a library. Through the introduction of his teacher, Lu Wenshu was able to meet such people and to borrow books. He would rise early in the morning as soon as it was light, and did his best to memorize the books in entirety. Still, the books always had to be returned at some point. He

though how wonderful it would be if he could copy the books, but his family had absolutely no materials with which to do that.

One day, Lu Wenshu was walking by a brook, tending sheep. Cattails were growing along the banks of the brook, and these suddenly inspired him. The leaves of the cattails were long and narrow. Perhaps he could use these in place of bamboo strips! He harvested many cattail leaves and cut them into the same size as bamboo strips, then dried these in the sun. When they were dry, he began to copy out a book, in careful neat handwriting. When he had the book copied, he gathered the leaves into one sheaf, and tied them together with string. His first "cattail-leaf book" was completed. Looking at this invention of his very own in his hands, Lu Wenshu was ecstatic: he owned a book!

Lu Wenshu became even more diligent in his studies after this. He looked everywhere for books, and copied them out as a cattail-leaf version. When he set out to herd sheep, he would have a book in his pocket. As the sheep grazed, he could read at any time. The years went by, and the cattail-leaf books that Lu Wemshu had copied filled his entire room and he became a veritable young scholar.

During the Western Han Period, the government began to pay attention to and abide by legal precedents. Many of the books that Lu Wenshu had copied out were about the law. He therefore decided to use this learning he had amassed to try and make a living. He first

served as a low-level administrator, as he continued his study of the law. Later, any questions in the county to do with legal matters were referred to him, and he was always able to supply a satisfactory answer. Above the county level in China at the time came the level of "jun," or prefecture. Once the head of the prefecture discovered his erudition, he promoted him and brought him to the prefectural seat. There, Lu Wenshu began studying works of history as well as law, and

many classics. He became an administrator who not only was versed in the law but had broad scholarship. In addition, he was conscientious in all he did, was honest, and disciplined, and his fame spread far and wide.

Several years later, Lu Wenshu's fame also came to the attention of the Emperor. The Emperor promoted him to serve in the Central government. From his own personal experience, Lu Wenshu felt very deeply about the injustices and the inadequacies of the prevailing system of law. He submitted a petition to the Emperor Han Xuandi, pointing out that the current legal system was mercilessly severe, that many people were put to death or had their hands or feet cut off, that officials beat prisoners at will and punished in advance of the trials, and that, under such circumstances, who wouldn't deliver a false confession? He asked for a full revision of the legal system. These recommendations met with Emperor Han Xuandi's approval and were put into effect, substantially reducing the hardships visited on common people. Lu Wenshu later served as head of the equivalent of the Supreme Court, but he never forgot the lessons he had learned from his "cattail-leaf books."

车胤囊萤与孙康映雪

原文：

rú náng yíng
如 囊 萤，

rú yìng xuě
如 映 雪，

jiā suī pín
家 虽 贫，

xué bú chuò
学 不 辍 。

故事：

　　古代没有电灯，到了晚上，人们就点起油灯照明。但有人买不起灯油，又想利用晚上的时间读书学习，怎么办呢？中国东晋（317—420）时候的车胤（yìn）和孙康各自找到了解决这个矛盾的办法。

　　车胤小时候就聪明好学，勤奋读书。他的父亲在郡的长官手下任职，这位长官见到车胤之后，对他父亲说："这个孩子将来会使你们家获得荣耀，你应该让他专门读书深造。"车胤的父亲也希望把儿子培养成一个有前途的人，可是车家很穷，车胤白天要帮大人做事，晚上才有时间读书，家里常常没钱买灯油，车胤为此而深感苦恼。

　　一个夏天的晚上，他从外面回来，发现草丛中有许多萤火虫一闪一闪地在飞。他心里一动，这些萤火虫的光可不可以用来读书呢？他捉了几十只萤火虫，装在白纱布缝制的口袋里挂起来，高兴地发现，这盏"灯"虽然不够亮，但确实可以用来照明读书。从此，他经常借着萤光读书，充分利用了晚上的时间。

　　车胤后来成为有名的学者，还担任过多个政府的重要职务，深受同时代人的尊重。现在，在他家乡有一所中学以他

的名字命名，以弘扬他的学习精神。

孙康生活的年代跟车胤差不多，小时候也是个热爱学习的孩子，常常感到时间不够用。可是因为家境贫寒，他买不起灯油，天黑之后便没办法看书了。特别是到了冬天，黑夜时间比较长，他不想把时间都用来睡觉，而想着怎么借用一点光亮来学习。

有一天晚上，他从睡梦中醒来，忽然发现从窗外透进了微弱的光。他起身开门一看，原来外面下了一场大雪，屋顶、地上、树上到处都是积雪。窗子透进的光，原来就是雪地所反射的月光。孙康想，既然这雪地的反光可以射进窗子里，那么是不是可以借着它来看书呢？他跑回屋里取出一本书，对着雪地的反光一看，果然能看清楚。他为找到了可以免费借用的光亮而兴奋，赶紧穿好衣服，跑到院子里来读书。

从这以后，孙康天天盼着下雪，因为这样他就不必为没有灯油而发愁了。他在冰天雪地里看书，饱受寒风之苦，但一点儿也不觉得辛苦。多年之后，他终于成为很有成就和名望的学者。

Che Yin Catches Lightning Bugs, and Sun Kang Reflects Snowlight

Without electricity in ancient times, people lit oil lamps when it became too dark to see. Many could not afford to buy the oil for such lamps, however, and after night fell there was little they could do. Two people who lived during the Dong Jin (Eastern Jin) Period (317–420) found ingenious ways to deal with this problem. One was Che Yin, and the other was Sun Kang.

As a small boy, Che Yin was clever and loved to study. His father served under the head of the Prefecture, who took note of the precocious Che Yin. One day, he said to the father, "This boy will bring glory to your house one day. You should let him focus on studying, let him achieve something." Che Yin's father would have liked to do that, let his son grow up as someone with a future, but the family was poor and Che Yin was forced to work for others all day. Only at night could he dedicate any time to study. Since there was rarely any money for lamp oil, Che Yin began to think about what he might do for a reading light.

One summer's evening, as he was coming home, he saw the spar-

kling light of many little fireflies in the darkness. Struck by a thought, he wondered if they might not produce enough light for him to read by. He caught a few dozen and put them in a bag made of white gauze, which he then tied overhead in his room. To his delight, he discovered that although the light was not brilliant by any means, it was sufficient for him to read by. From then on, he used the night hours well, to study.

In later days, Che Yin did indeed become a famous scholar. He was highly respected by contemporaries and served in a number of responsible positions. Today, a middle school has been named in his honor in his home town, to commemorate the spirit with which he sought to learn.

Sun Kang lived at roughly the same time as Che Yin. As a young child, he too loved learning and often felt there was not enough time. Since the family lacked the money for lamp oil, however, when night fell there was no way for him to read. Winters were especially hard, since the days were short and the nights were long. He would much have preferred to study than to waste his time in sleeping.

One night, he woke up from a dream and saw a soft light coming in through the window. Getting up to look out the door, he found that a snow had fallen and the eaves, the ground, the trees, were all covered in a layer of whiteness. The light that had come through the window

had been reflected moonlight, shining off the snow. Since this light re-
flected from the ground came all the way in through the window, Sun
Kang wondered if it might perhaps be enough for him to read by. He
ran to get a book and let the reflected light fall on it—sure enough, it
was possible to read. To be able to use the snow-light, for free, made

him deliriously happy. He quickly got dressed and ran out into the yard, where he began to read.

From this day on, Sun Kang hoped daily for snow. He would not have to worry about not having the money for oil. Whenever it snowed, he bundled up and spent the night hours reading, braving the wind and the cold. Many years later, he too became a famous and accomplished scholar.

朱买臣砍柴不忘读书

原文：

rú fù xīn　　　rú guà jiǎo
如 负 薪 ，　　如 挂 角 。

shēn suī láo　　yóu kǔ zhuó
身 虽 劳 ，　　犹 苦 卓 。

故事：

　　西汉的汉武帝（前157—前87）时候，江苏苏州有个叫朱买臣的人，父母很早就去世了，没留下什么财产。他只好到山上去砍柴，靠卖柴的钱维持生活，日子过得很艰苦。

　　尽管处境这样糟糕，朱买臣却很有报负，认为自己将来一定能成就一番事业。他喜欢读书学习，上山打柴时也经常把书带在身边。工作累了的时候，他就拿出书来读，把这当作休息。担着柴回家的路上，他也一直背诵书中的内容。

　　后来朱买臣结婚成家，仍然卖柴为生，夫妻二人有时穷得连饭都吃不上。更让妻子觉得难堪的是，朱买臣一直不放弃读书求学的想法，在周围人的眼里，他变成了一个古怪的

人。每次到集市上去卖柴的时候，朱买臣总是一边担着柴走路，一边大声地念着普通人听不懂的文章。妻子劝他不要这样做，但朱买臣念书的声音反而更大了。

有一次，两人又为此而发生不愉快，妻子很生气，回到家之后，就提出要离开。朱买臣对她说："我将来一定会受到朝廷重用的，你跟着我也辛苦这么多年了，再忍耐几年，我就能报答你。"妻子冷笑着说："你现在都四十多岁了，还要等

到什么时候？等你富贵的时候，我恐怕早就饿死在路边的沟里面了！"她终于还是离朱买臣而去了。

妻子离开之后，朱买臣并没有灰心丧气。他坚持一边砍柴养活自己，一边挤出时间来读书和写作。他的一些文章流传到京城里，得到人们的赞赏。

几年后，朱买臣得到一个机会，作为地方官员的临时随从来到西汉王朝的都城长安（今陕西西安）。正好他的一个同乡在朝廷任职，是汉武帝所宠幸的人，这同乡就向汉武帝推荐了他。汉武帝召见朱买臣，交谈之后，觉得他是个有学识、有才干的人，就让他留在朝中做官。朱买臣终于可以发挥自己自己的特长，他还写了一些华丽的文章献给汉武帝，汉武帝大加赞赏。

后来，汉武帝又任命朱买臣为他家乡的地方长官，让他风风光光地回去。家乡的官员和老百姓们听说新长官来了，都跑出来迎接。有人惊讶地发现，这位新长官原来就是当年集市上那位一边走路一边大声念书的卖柴人！这个时候，朱买臣已经五十岁了，但他的事业才刚刚开始。

Zhu Maichen Chops Wood but Does Not Forget to Study

At the time of the Emperor Han Wudi (157–87 BCE), a man named Zhu Maichen lived in Suzhou, Jiangsu. His father died when he was young and left no inheritance. With no other support, Zhu Maichen began to cut wood in the forests and sell it for firewood as a way to make a living. His life was bitterly difficult.

Nevertheless, Zhu Maichen had the feeling that one day he would be able to accomplish great things. He liked to study, and when he went into the mountains to chop wood, he would always take a book along. When he took a break, he would draw out the book and read it as a way to relax. While carrying the wood back along the road to town, he would recite aloud from the book that he had read during the day.

As time went on, Zhu Maichen got married and started a family, but he still made a living by chopping wood and the family was very poor. They often did not have enough to eat. This bothered the wife, but what bothered her even more was that Zhu Maichen did not give up the habit of reading. In the eyes of all those around, he had become a very strange man. When he went to market with his wood suspended

from a peddler's pole carried on his shoulders, he would chant memorized texts aloud in a loud voice, texts that nobody else could understand. His wife would implore him not to do this, which only made him chant the louder.

One day, the two yet again argued over this matter and the wife became angry. When they got home, she announced that she was leaving. Zhu Maichen said to her, "I am going to be asked to serve the court in the future, and I'll be rich. You have been together with me through all these poor years, have a little more patience for a few years and I will

be able to compensate you for all the hard times." With a cold laugh, the wife replied, "You are already over forty years old. How long am I going to have to wait? By the time you are rich and famous, I will be dead, starved to death in that ditch over by the road!" In the end, she left him.

Zhu Maichen was not discouraged after his wife's departure. He lost none of his usual energy. He simply kept on cutting wood and using whatever time he could find to read and to write. Some of his compositions made it up to the capital city, where they were noticed and

highly regarded.

A few years later, Zhu Maichen's opportunity came knocking. He was asked to serve as a temporary aide to the local official on his trip to the capital of Chang'an (today's Xi'an in Shaanxi), to the Western Han emperor's court. By chance, one of his fellow countrymen was serving as an official in the court and was in fact one of the people greatly favored and trusted by the Emperor. This fellow countryman put Zhu Maichen forward as someone the Emperor should employ. The Emperor Han Wudi had an audience with Zhu Maichen and was favorably impressed with his scholarship and his talent. Zhu Maichen was asked to stay on at the court. At last, Zhu Maichen was able to make use of his better qualities, and he wrote some beautiful compositions as offerings to the Emperor, who was appreciative.

In due course, the Emperor appointed Zhu Maichen to be the senior official back in his old home town, and he sent him back in style. All the local officials and people came out to welcome their new official. Some were amazed to discover that it was Zhu Maichen, the very fellow who had once hauled wood down the path as he recited the classics out loud! By this time, Zhu Maichen was already over fifty, and yet his life's work had really just begun.

苏洵发愤读书

原文：

sū lǎo quán，　èr shí qī
苏 老 泉，　二 十 七，

shǐ fā fèn，　dú shū jí
始 发 愤，　读 书 籍。

bǐ jì lǎo，　yóu huǐ chí
彼 既 老，　犹 悔 迟；

ěr xiǎo shēng　yí zǎo sī
尔 小 生，　宜 早 思。

故事：

　　北宋的时候,四川有一个叫苏洵（xún）的人，天姿聪明，擅长辩论，很少有人说得过他。但他不喜欢读书，成天东游西荡。十九岁结婚以后，仍然如此。

　　苏洵的妻子程氏比他小一岁，受过良好的教育。她的父母家富有，而丈夫家比较贫穷，婚后生活艰难，对此她并不在意。但看到丈夫无所事事的样子，她非常忧心，常常闷闷不乐。她性情温和，从不为此事而当面指责丈夫。当时苏洵

　　的哥哥已经考取了进士，程氏就对丈夫说："看到哥哥受人尊敬的情形，我也觉得脸上很有光彩呢！"聪明的苏洵当然知道妻子的意思，但他不愿放弃自己原来的生活方式。

　　再后来，他们有了一个儿子。儿子长大了，苏洵不喜欢读书，当然也不会特别督促儿子学习；程氏就主动担当起了儿子的老师，教他读书识字。有一天，儿子觉得学习很辛苦，就对母亲说："妈妈，为什么我要在书房里学习，而爸爸就可以不用学习，到处跑呢？"程氏叹了一口气，说："如果你将来跟爸爸一样，我会很难过！"乖巧的儿子赶紧安慰母亲，答应好好学习。看着儿子，程氏觉得很欣慰；可是想到丈夫已经

二十七岁了，仍然一事无成，她不由得又叹息起来。

苏洵无意间听到了母子之间这番对话，很受震动。自从结婚以来，妻子对贫穷的生活毫无怨言，却因为自己的所作所为，几乎没有开心的时候。想到这里，苏洵觉得很惭愧。

第二天一早，程氏照常带着儿子到书房学习，却惊奇地发现，书房里早有人了，原来是丈夫苏洵正在里面整理图书和纸笔呢。苏洵说："儿子也到了求学上进的年龄，从此之后，就由我这个当父亲的来履行教育孩子的职责吧！"程氏没想到丈夫居然有了这么大的转变，虽然不明白其中的原因，但她看到丈夫脸上那种前所未有的高昂神气，不禁露出了灿烂的笑容。

从此，苏家的书房里就每天传出父子二人朗朗的读书声。程氏忙着做琐碎的家务，但她觉得很幸福。再后来，苏洵和程氏又有了一个儿子。这样，在书房里每天读书的就变成了三个人。

苏洵和两个儿子苏轼（shì）（即苏东坡）、苏辙（zhé）后来都以擅长写文章和学识渊博而著称，并且都考取了进士，被人们合称为"三苏"。有人选出中国古代最有名的八个散文家，称为"唐宋八大家"，苏氏父子就占据了其中的三个名额。

Su Xun Reforms, and Starts to Study

During the Northern Song Period, in Sichuan, a man named Su Xun had an innate intelligence and the ability to out-debate anyone, but at the same time he had no interest in reading books or learning things. He spent all his time roaming around. He did not change his ways after marrying at the age of nineteen.

Su Xun's wife was one year younger than he was. Named Cheng Shi, she came from a fine and educated family, fairly well-to-do, while Su Xun's family was rather poor. Life after marrying Su Xun was hard, but Cheng Shi did not mind this. She worried as she saw her husband's idle ways, but she kept it to herself. She was a gentle person by nature, and never criticized her husband for his behavior. At the time, Su Xun's elder brother had already passed the exam to be a jin-shi, and at that point she did say to her husband, "Seeing elder brother become such a respected person certainly does make me feel more respected too!" Su Xun was intelligent enough to know what she meant, but he was not willing to change his lifestyle.

Still later, the couple had a son. As the son grew up, since his father did not like to study, naturally he did not encourage his son to

study either. Cheng Shi decided to become the teacher of the child herself. She taught him how to read. One day, as the son was feeling it was really a lot of work to study, he asked his mother, "Mama, why should I have to study indoors, when Papa can run around outside?" Cheng Shi sighed and said, "It will make me very sad if you grow up to be like your father." The clever child quickly comforted his mother and responded that he would study hard. Cheng Shi felt better looking at this child, but when she recalled that her husband was already twenty-seven, and had done nothing in life, she drew another long sigh.

By chance, Su Xun overheard this conversation, and was very moved by it. Since marrying, his wife had never had a word of complaint about their poverty-stricken life. On the contrary, due to her abilities there had never been a moment of unhappiness. Thinking this over, Su Xun felt even more ashamed.

The next day, early, Cheng Shi went to teach her son in the study as usual, but to her amazement she found that the room was already occupied, indeed by none other than her husband. He was bustling around getting books, papers, brushes in order. Su Xun said to her, "Our son is already of an age to study. From now on, as the father, I am going to take over the responsibility of carrying out the child's education." Cheng Shi could not believe that her husband had undergone such a great transformation. Although she did not understand what was

behind the change, she could see the resolution on his face and she couldn't help but feel a glow of happiness as well.

From this day on, the voices of father and son could be heard every day issuing from the study, reading books aloud. Cheng Shi busied herself with housework, and she felt extremely fortunate. Later, Su Xun and Cheng Shi had another son and the study soon rang with the voices of three people reading and reciting.

Su Xun and his two sons, Su Shi (that is, Su Dongpo) and Su Zhe later were to excel in the art of composition, as well as to be renowned for their erudition. All three, moreover, passed the imperial exam that allowed them to be awarded with the degree called jin-shi. They became known as the "three Su's." Eight names are included in the "Eight masters of the Tang and Song dynasties," premier names in all of ancient China for their talent in writing prose. Among those eight names, three are occupied by the three Su's.

Tales of Virtue

美德故事

窦禹钧教育五子

原文：

dòu yān shān　　yǒu yì fāng
窦燕山，有义方，

jiào wǔ zǐ　　míng jù yáng
教五子，名俱扬。

故事：

"赵普读《论语》"那个故事中提到，宋太祖向两个学识渊博的大臣询问年号"乾德"的问题，从他们那里得到了正确答案。这两个大臣中有一个叫窦仪，宋太祖认为他的品德、才能、学识足以担任宰相，可惜他五十多岁就去世了，没能担任这个职务。令人惊讶的是，窦仪的四个弟弟也都是很杰出的人物，都在朝廷里担任重要职务。兄弟五人取得这样的成就并不是偶然的，因为他们都受到父亲窦禹钧的良好教育和影响。

窦禹钧的家乡在中国北方的燕（yān）山一带，因此后人称他为窦燕山。他生活的五代时期（907—960），政治非常动

乱，几乎天天都在打仗。但他认为，不能因此就放弃对孩子的教育。他家教很严格，要求孩子们所作所为首先都要合乎正义，讲道理。

窦禹钧不但这样教导儿子们，而且他自己就是这样做的。窦禹钧很有学问，也担任过比较高的官职。但最重要的是，他一生中做了很多慈善之事，比如有的年轻人到了结婚

的年龄，却因贫穷而不能婚嫁，他就出钱替他们办婚事；有的穷人去世了没有钱下葬，他就资助丧葬费用。他用各种方式资助别人的事例，数都数不清。更有意义的是，他建立了实行免费教育的学校。他在自己家的空地上建造了几十间教室，收集数千卷图书，聘请一些德高望重的老师来教课，帮助那些因贫寒而上不起学的孩子完成学业。他自己的生活则很俭朴，每年的收入，除了留下家庭必要的生活费用之外，都拿出来救助别人。

窦仪五兄弟就是在这样的学校里接受了教育，父亲的言论和行为，成为他们最好的榜样。他们学业优秀，品德也很高尚，远近的人们都把窦家视为模范家庭。当时，国家通过科举考试选拔人才，每次选出的人很少，而窦仪兄弟五人先后都通过考试而成为国家栋梁，这在中国历史上是极为罕见的。他们进入朝廷后，仍然遵循父亲所教导的做人原则，既正直勤勉，又很有修养，赢得了从皇帝到普通人的尊敬。窦仪去世后，宋太祖沉痛地对身边的人说："上天为什么这么早就把窦仪从我身边夺走呢？"他还多次称赞窦仪几个弟弟的人品和才学。

窦禹钧活了八十多岁，当时有一位名人写了一首诗送给他，说他就像一棵长寿而枝叶仍然茂盛的老树；而他的五个儿子，就好比五根芳香远飘的丹桂枝条。

Dou Yujun Educates His Five Sons

The story about Zhao Pu reading *the Analects* has already mentioned two scholarly ministers who were able to provide Song Taizu with the correct answer about whether or not his reign name had already been taken by someone else. One of the two officials, who knew that "Qian De" had already been used, was named Dou Yi. Song Taizu felt that his character, his abilities and knowledge fully qualified him to serve as Prime Minister. Unfortunately, he died at the age of slightly over fifty and was not able to take on this responsibility. What amazes people is that Dou Yi's four younger brothers were also outstanding men, each serving the court in important positions. The accomplishments of the five brothers was not accidental, but rather the result of their excellent education as provided by their father, Dou Yujun.

Dou Yujun's homeland was in the region of the Yan mountains (Yanshan), in northwestern China. He is often called Dou Yanshan as a result. He lived during the Five Dynasties period (907–960), when the political situation was extremely turbulent and warfare was constant. He did not feel that one should abandon a child's education just because of that. His methods were strict, and children were required to

do everything on the basis of honest and proper dealings with people.

Dou Yujun not only taught his children to behave in this manner, but he himself led by example. He was highly educated and had served as senior official in a number of capacities, but the most important

thing about him was his philanthropic activity. Throughout his life, he bestowed gifts on people who needed them, young people who needed enough money to get married, poor people who needed money to bury a relative, and so on. Through his munificence, he supported countless numbers of people. Even more significant, he instituted tuition-free schools to carry out local education. In a vacant part of his own property, he built a school with several tens of classrooms, and collected several thousand books as a library. He invited visionary and ethical men to come serve as teachers, and helped those students who were too poor to attend school to finish their education. His own life was extremely simple and austere. Except for what he needed for his own household and daily life, his entire income was spent on helping others.

It was in this kind of school that Dou Yi and his brothers were educated. Their father's words and behavior became their most important role model. Their ethical qualities and their scholarship were so impressive that all people looked up to the Dou household as the ideal family. At this time, the country was just instituting the "ke-ju" system of imperial examinations, which selected people on the basis of exam results. The number selected every time was very small, but all five brothers not only passed but became "pillars of the State." This was something very seldom seen in the annals of Chinese his-

tory. After entering the court, they continued to adhere to principles of how to behave as an upright human being, principles that their father had instilled in them. The principles included being honorable, highly cultivated, and able to win the respect of both the Emperor and the common man. After Dou Yi died, the emperor Song Taizu is known to have said in grief, "Why did heaven have to snatch Dou Yi from my side?!" The emperor applauded the character and talents of the four brothers a number of times after that as well.

Dou Yujun lived to be more than eighty years old. A poem written about him in his later years likened him to a big old tree whose branches and leaves were still flourishing. His five sons were likened to twigs of the orange osmanthus, whose fragrance floated to distant regions of the country in the breezes.

黄香温席扇枕

原文：

xiāng jiǔ líng néng wēn xí
香 九 龄 ， 能 温 席 ，

xiào yú qīn suǒ dāng zhí
孝 于 亲 ， 所 当 执 。

故事：

　　黄香是中国东汉时期（25—220）的一位名人。他的家乡在现在的湖北省安陆市，父亲做过低级别的官员，家里生活并不富裕。黄香聪慧早熟，很小的时候就主动帮助父母做家务，以减轻他们的劳累，让他们心情舒畅。

　　冬天的夜晚，黄香读书时手脚都冻得冰凉。他想，这么冷的天，辛苦了一天的爸爸妈妈怎能睡得好呢？那个时候，普通人家都缺乏取暖的设备。于是他悄悄跑到父母的房间，躺到被子里，用自己的体温使被子温暖了之后，才去请父母来休息。开始的时候父母还奇怪，为什么床铺变得暖和而舒服。当他们知道儿子的做法时，非常感动。

在黄香的家乡，夏天特别湿热，而且蚊子、苍蝇等打扰人们睡眠的小昆虫很多。黄香的父母为了降温和驱赶蚊虫，只好不停地摇着扇子，但仍然翻来覆去睡不着。怎么办呢？黄香又开始悄悄行动了。当大家还在院子里乘凉的时候，他早早回到闷热的屋子里，向枕头、席子使劲挥动扇子，希望屋子里能凉快一些；又努力把帐子里的蚊虫赶走，这样父母就能睡个安稳觉。看着热得浑身是汗的小黄香，父母十分心疼。

黄香九岁时，母亲生了重病，卧床不起。小黄香日夜守护在病床前，尽力照顾她，但母亲还是不幸病故了，黄香非常悲痛。母亲去世后，因为家里没有仆人，黄香担心父亲也生病，就特别用心地照顾他，承担了很多家务。

在关心、照顾父亲的同时，黄香并没有耽误学习。他博览群书，十二岁时便看了很多书，写出了内容充实的文章。看到和听说过他的人，都称赞他是个孝敬长辈、勤奋学习的好孩子。地方上的长官听说之后，召见了他，交谈之后，对他大为欣赏。

当时的皇帝是汉章帝，非常重视人才，听说了黄香的名声之后，让黄香到京城洛阳去见他。汉章帝敬重黄香的为人和才学，就让他留在自己身边担任官职，准许他到皇家藏书的地方学习。黄香刻苦研读各种典籍，学识和见解更加出众。过了一段时间，他挂念远在家乡的父亲，汉章帝便同意他回家乡去探望。但不久就又把他叫回京城。在一次皇室的聚会上，

　　汉章帝将他介绍给众人，说："这位就是天下无双的名士黄香。"大家都以敬慕的目光看着他。

　　黄香后来担任了相当于宰相的高官，他对待公务犹如对待父母一样，十分认真、用心，关心民众的疾苦。他的儿子黄琼后来也当上高官，同样因为廉洁、正直而天下驰名。

Huang Xiang Practices
Fanning the Pillow

Huang Xiang lived during the Eastern Han Period in China (25
–220). His home was in what is now Anlu City in Hubei Province,

where his father served as a minor official. The family was not well-to-do. Huang Xiang grew up a precocious child who early on helped his parents with chores as a natural and voluntary thing to do. It not only enlightened their load but made him happy as well.

One cold winter's night, when Huang Xiang was reading, he realized that his feet were so very cold that his parents must be cold and tired as well. After working hard all day, how could they possibly get a good nights' sleep in a freezing-cold bed. Back in those days, the houses of normal people did not have any heating apparatus. Huang Xiang quietly stole into his parents' room and crawled into their bed, in order to warm it with his body. Then he asked his parents to sleep well. At first, they found it strange that their bed should be so nicely warm, and then were highly moved when they realized they realized the thoughtfulness of their son.

The countryside in Huang Xiang's homeland is very hot and humid in the summer, and mosquitos, flies and all kinds of little insects make it hard to sleep. Huang Xiang's parents used to try to fan themselves as they went to bed, but this only made them toss and turn all the more. Huang Xiang again took action. When everyone was still out in the yard, trying to stay cool, he went to the hot bedroom and fanned the pillow and the bedding like mad, trying to cool it off. He also drove all of the mosquitos out of the mosquito net so that when

his parents came to bed they could sleep peacefully. Seeing their son covered with sweat, trying to make them cool, made his parents love him all the more.

When Huang Xiang was nine years old, his mother took to bed with a grave illness. Little Huang Xiang attended her day and night, doing all he could to make her comfortable. When she died, he was inconsolable. After his mother's death, as there were no servants to do the chores, he took on all the tasks that his mother had done in order to ensure that his father would not become ill as well from all the extra work.

Even in the course of looking after his father, Huang Xiang did not neglect his studies. He read broadly and by the age of twelve had not only read many books but composed a number of pieces of prose that could be said to have real substance. Everyone who knew him or had heard about him said that he was an extremely filial and also studious child. When the local magistrate heard about him, he asked to meet him and was highly impressed.

The emperor at that time was Han Zhangdi. This emperor greatly supported people with talent, and when he heard about Huang Xiang, for his fame had spread, he asked Huang Xiang to come to the capital city of Anyang for an audience with him. Having ascertained his talents and his general comportment, he asked him to stay in the city

and serve at his side as an official. He also permitted him to use the imperial library for his studies. Huang Xiang industriously studied all kinds of classics and his erudition became even more outstanding. After a while, however, he began to miss his father, back in the distant homeland. Han Zhangdi allowed him to return home to see how things were, but soon asked him to return to the capital. At their next meeting, the emperor introduced him to people he had assembled by saying, "This is the incomparable Huang Xiang, unique under heaven." Everyone then regarded him with great respect.

After Huang Xiang served in a position that was equivalent in ancient days to Prime Minister, he treated public affairs with the same diligence that he had attended his parents. He was conscientious, careful, and cared about the wellbeing of the people. His son, Huang qióng, later also ascended to high position and was similarly honest and upright, with the result that his name too spread throughout the land.

孔融让梨

原文：

róng sì suì　　néng ràng lí
融 四 岁 ， 能 让 梨 ，

tì yú zhǎng　　yí xiān zhī
弟 于 长 ， 宜 先 知 。

故事：

　　生活在东汉末年的孔融，是现在的山东省曲阜市人。他出生在中国最有名的书香世家，是孔子的第二十世孙。孔融以文章和学问著称，而中国人至今仍然津津乐道的，是他小时候的事情。

　　孔融兄弟一共七人，他排行第六，上面有五个哥哥，下面还有一个弟弟。七兄弟彼此之间非常友爱。孔融四岁时，有一次家里得到一些梨子，妈妈让孩子们一起来吃。孩子们看见香甜多汁的梨子都很高兴，因为梨子有的大，有的小，妈妈就让最小的孔融和弟弟先挑选。孔融看了看，挑出一个最小的，把大一些的梨子让给了弟弟和哥哥们。

　　正好爸爸经过他们身边，看见这情形，就问他："妈妈让你先挑选，你为什么挑了个最小的呢？"孔融回答："我年龄小，不应该吃大的。"爸爸指着最小的儿子又问："弟弟不是比你小吗，为什么你又把大梨留给他呢？"孔融答道："他是弟弟，我是哥哥，应该照顾他呀！"

　　爸爸听了孔融的回答，觉得他聪明而又懂事，心里很高兴，但还是故意问："这么好吃的梨子，大家都想多吃几口，难道你就不想吗？"孔融说："我们是兄弟，感情好

得不分彼此，哥哥和弟弟获得了快乐，就等于我也获得了快乐。"听了孔融的话，哥哥、弟弟也纷纷谦让，还把最好吃的梨子拿给爸爸妈妈尝。看到这种情形，孔融的父母十分欣慰。

孔融十岁的时候，跟随父亲到首都洛阳，拜会名望很高的李膺（yīng）。孔融先跑到李家门前，守门人因为他是个孩子，不肯为他通报。孔融说："我跟李先生家有很亲近的关系。"守门人只得让他进去。李膺不认识他，就问："请问你的祖父或者父亲跟我有交情吗？"孔融回答："我的祖上是孔子，先生您的祖上是老子（本名李耳），孔子曾经拜老子为师，他们两位是这样的关系，那我家与您家不就世世代代都有交情吗？"在座的人听了都哈哈大笑，李膺也被孔融的解释逗乐了，将他当作客人对待。孔融的父亲来了，李膺夸奖说，这个孩子将来一定会成为了不起的人物。

孔融成年后果然成为一代名士，在文学和儒学方面都很有成就。

Kong Rong Offers
the Best Pears to Others

Kong Rong lived during the latter part of the Eastern Han, in Qufu City in what is now the province of Shandong. He was born into the most illustrious of all scholarly families in China, namely the Kong family. He was the twenty-second generation of Kong descendants, after Confucius. Kong Rong became famous for his literary achievements and scholarship, but the thing most people remember him for today relates to tales of his childhood.

He was sixth among seven brothers, with five older and one younger, all of whom got along extremely well. One time, the family was given some pears and the mother of the children wanted them all to share them. The children gazed at the pears, mouths watering, and noticed that some were larger and some were smaller. Kong Rong was four years old at the time. His mother asked the two youngest boys to choose first. Kong Rong chose the smallest of the pears and allowed both his older brothers and his younger brother to take the bigger ones.

Just then, his father happened to pass by and noticed this. He asked, "You were allowed to go first, so why did you choose the smallest?" Kong Rong answered, "I'm younger, so I shouldn't have a larger

pear." His father pointed out that his little brother was even younger, so Kong Rong then said, "He is Little Brother, I am Older Brother to him, so naturally I need to look after him!"

The father was quite pleased with this but he continued to question his son. "Such delicious pears, and everyone wants a few more bites, don't you feel the same way?" Kong Rong responded, "We are all brothers, and don't distinguish between what's yours and what's mine. When my brothers are happy, that means I'm happy too." Hearing all of this, the brothers all allowed others better pears as well and offered

up the best pears to their mother and father.

When Kong Rong was ten years old, he accompanied his father to the capital city of Luoyang to pay a formal call on the famous personage Li Ying. Kong Rong got to the door first, and the guard there would not announce him, since he was just a child. Kong Rong declared, "I have a very close relationship with Mr. Li's family," so the guard had no choice but to let him in. Li Ying did not recognize Kong Rong, however, and instead asked, "Please let me know, did your father or grandfather have some connection to me?" Kong Rong replied, "My ancestor was Confucius, and Sir, your ancestor was Lao-zi (whose original name was Li Er). Confucius regarded Lao-zi as his teacher. That was the relationship, so our families have had a connection through many generations." Those sitting nearby laughed at this, and Li Ying himself was also pleased with the explanation. He treated little Kong Rong as an honored guest. When Kong Rong's father arrived, Li Ying boasted that the child would certainly be a great man in the future.

Indeed, when he grew up, Kong Rong became "one in a generation" in the fields of literature and the Ru-school of philosophy.

Tales of Talants
人才故事

老子出关

原文：

wǔ zǐ zhě　　yǒu xún yáng
五子者，有荀扬，

wén zhōng zǐ　　jí lǎo zhuāng
文中子，及老庄。

故事：

　　老子是中国古代伟大的哲学家、思想家，道家学派的创始人。他的思想影响中国达数千年之久，而且传播到了中国以外的不少地方。关于他的生平和他不朽的著作《道德经》，有一些神奇的传说。

　　据史书记载，老子名叫李耳，又叫老聃（dān），所以人们尊称他为老子。他跟孔子一样，生活在春秋时期，比孔子年长一些。他长期在周王手下担任管理藏书的史官之职，熟悉从前的礼法制度，孔子曾特意前来向他请教这方面的问题。除了向孔子介绍礼制之外，老子还讲了许多为人处事的道理。孔子告别老子之后，对学生们说："那乘着风云而飞上天的龙，我

们很难完全了解它，老子不也是这样高深莫测吗？"

晚年时候，老子见周王朝日益衰败，诸侯之间经常
发生战争，于是决定隐居到偏僻遥远的地方去。他辞去官

职，骑着一头黑色的牛，离开都城洛阳向西走，打算到西边的秦国去。

这一天，他来到了一个叫函谷关的关口。老子的外貌和风度很特别，这引起了负责把守关口的官员尹喜的注意。尹喜也是一个很有学问的人，而且喜欢钻研一些在当时人看来很神秘的东西。他拦住老子，跟他交谈了一会儿，才发现这位老人就是大名鼎鼎的老子。听说老子想远走他乡，尹喜觉得很惋惜，劝老子留下来，但老子去意已定。尹喜又恳求说："既然您一定要离开，我也不能强硬地阻拦。但您这一走，我们就再也不容易见到了。可不可以答应我一个请求，在这儿住一段时间，把您思想学说的要点写下来留给我们。"禁不住他再三恳请，老子于是答应停留几天，写一本著作。

老子一边思索，一边用简洁的语言记录下自己的思想和学说。过了一段时间，终于写成了五千多字的著作，分成上下两篇，上篇第一句谈"道"，下篇第一句谈"德"，所以这本书被称为《道德经》，又叫《老子》。在这本书里，老子探讨了从宇宙天地到人世间各种现象之间的复杂关系，其中许多话都深奥而不容易理解。

老子写完这本书，就骑着牛离开了函谷关，向西而去，谁也不知道他后来到底去了哪里。人们对他后来的行踪有多种猜测，一些民间故事更是将他描述成地位崇高的神仙。

Lao-zi Goes over the Pass

Lao-zi was not only a very great philosopher and thinker in ancient China, but he founded the school of philosophy known as Daoism. The influence of his thinking has been perpetuated for thousands of years within China and has also been transmitted to many places outside China. There is one particularly marvelous legend about his life and his masterpiece, *the Dao De Jing*.

According to historical records, the actual name of Lao-zi was Li Er, although he was also called Lao Dan. Everyone used the respectful form of address in calling him Lao-zi. Like Kong-zi (Confucius), he lived at the time of the Spring and Autumn Period. He served for a long period under the King of Chou, as the official in charge of records, and he was very familiar with the former system of rites and rituals. Confucius specifically visited him to ask his advice on these matters. In addition to introducing the ritual system to Confucius, Lao-zi also described many principles of how to "be a person," that is, how properly to comport oneself and handle one's dealings with others, and how to manage affairs. After parting, Confucius said to one of his students, "It is hard for us to fully understand the dragon, who rides the

winds and the clouds, and Lao-zi is just as high and abstruse!"

In his later years, seeing that the Chou dynasty was likely to collapse any day, that wars among the princes were occurring with ever greater frequency, Lao-zi decided to take himself off to a remote, isolated place to live as a hermit. He resigned his position and, riding on a black water buffalo, he left the capital city of Luoyang and headed west. He planned to get to the Qin State on the western frontier.

On the day in question, he arrived at a pass called "Hangu Pass." There he drew the attention of the man guarding the pass, since Lao-zi's appearance and manner were rather special. The guard, Yin Xi, was a man of great learning, and he particularly liked to learn about things that seemed very mysterious back then. He began talking with Lao-zi and soon found out that this was the Lao-zi of ultimate fame that everyone had heard about. He knew that Lao-zi intended to move to distant regions, which he thought most unfortunate, so he tried to persuade Lao-zi to stay right there. Lao-zi was determined to go. Yin Xi then said, "I can see that you are going to leave, and I cannot force you to stay, but before you go would you honor my one request. Stay here for just a short time and write down the main aspects of your philosophy, and leave them behind for me." Unable to stop Yin Xi from asking this most earnestly, over and over again, Lao-zi decided to stop there for a few days and write for a while.

He thought things over and then, in simple and direct language, wrote down his own way of thinking and his philosophy. In a short time, what he had written totaled more than 5,000 words, and was divided into two parts, first and second. The first sentence of the first part talked about "Dao," while the first sentence of the second part talked about "De." Later, this book therefore came to be called *the Dao De Jing*, or *the Classic of Dao and De, the Way and the Virtue*. It sometimes is also called *Lao-zi*. In this book, Lao-zi explores the complex relationships among all phenomena, from the universe itself, to affairs among human beings, although much of the language is abstruse and not easy to understand.

Once Lao-zi had written this book, he got back on his water buffalo and left Han Gu Pass, headed on to the west. Nobody knows where he went after that. There are many conjectures as to what happened to him, and some folktales even say that he turned into a kind of lofty spirit.

庄子遁世

原文：

wǔ zǐ zhě　　yǒu xún yáng
五子者，有荀扬，

wén zhōng zǐ　　jí lǎo zhuāng
文中子，及老庄。

故事：

庄子（约前369—前286）本名叫庄周，生活在战国时期，是道家学派的另一位代表人物，与老子并称老庄。他喜欢逍遥自在的隐居生活，喜欢讽刺他看不惯的人物和现象。他和他的学生、追随者的著作汇编为《庄子》一书，这本书想象丰富，富有文学色彩，里面讲了不少跟庄子有关的故事，都流露出一种幽默的喜剧色彩。

有一天，庄子正在河边钓鱼，这时，楚国国王派来的两位官员找到他，说是奉楚王的命令来请庄子去做官。他们客气地说："我们的国王很重视您，想把国家的事情拜托给您，让您为此而劳累！"庄子拿着钓竿，看也不看他们一眼，说：

"我听说楚国有一只神龟，死了三千年了；国王把它用锦缎包好，放进竹制的箱子里，珍藏于祭祀的地方。你们说，这只龟是愿意这样死掉让人们重视他呢，还是愿意活着在烂泥里摇尾巴呢？"两位官员说："它愿意活着在烂泥里摇尾巴。"庄子说："那二位就回去吧！我也情愿在烂泥里摇尾巴。"说罢，继续专心地钓鱼，再也不搭理那两位使者。

庄子有一位老朋友叫惠子，两人因为见解不同，多次发

生争论。有一段时间，惠子得到梁王重用，做了主管国家大事的相国。庄子知道了这事，就前往梁国看望他。有一些人不知出于什么目的，在惠子面前说庄子的坏话："庄子这次到梁国来，恐怕是想取代你的地位，成为梁国的新相国。"惠子害怕失去自己的地位，于是听信了这种传言，命令部下在梁国都城搜捕庄子，找了三天三夜，也没见到庄子。其实庄子还在路上呢，他听说这种情形，并不逃避，仍然按原计划到都城里去看望惠子。

两人见面之后，庄子对惠子说："你知不知道，南方有一种高贵的鸟叫鹓雏（yuān chú）？它从南海飞到北海去，只有遇到梧桐树才停下来休息，除了竹子的果实，什么也不吃；除了甘甜的泉水，什么也不喝。它飞过某个地方时，正好有只猫头鹰找到一只腐臭的死老鼠；看见鹓雏从面前飞过，猫头鹰担心人家来跟它争那只腐鼠，于是仰起头怒视着鹓雏，发出不友好的声音。现在你是不是也因为你的梁国而要对我发出那种声音？"

惠子很惭愧，知道误解了庄子，于是两人之间又恢复了友情。庄子并没有停留很久，又返回山林里继续他的隐居生活。

Zhuang-zi Escapes the Troubled World

The original name of Zhuang-zi (369–286 BCE) was Zhuang Zhou. He lived during the Warring States Period and was a key person in the school of philosophy known as Daoism. He is often put together with Lao-zi; the two are often referred to as Lao-Zhuang. He enjoyed the free and unfettered life of a hermit and he enjoyed satirizing things and people. The works of Zhuang-zi and his students and followers were edited into a volume known as *Zhuang-zi*, which contains not only rich philosophy but is written in a beautifully literary style. It tells many stories relating to Zhuang-zi that also have a humorous touch to them.

One day, when Zhuang-zi was sitting by a river fishing, two officials that had been sent by the King of the State of Chu to find him informed him that they were ordered to bring him back to serve as an official in the court. They said very politely, "Our King has a very high regard for you and wants to authorize you to manage affairs of State, he hopes to burden you with this task!" Zhuang-zi kept on fishing, without even glancing at the officials. He said, "I've heard that the State of Chu has a sacred tortoise that has been dead three thousand

years. The King has wrapped him up in silks and put him into a box made of bamboo, which he keeps in a place for special rituals. Now tell me, do you think that this tortoise would rather be dead and in a place where people have high regard for him, or would he rather be alive and dragging his tail in the mud?"

The two officials answered, "He would rather be dragging his tail in the mud."

"Then you two run along!" said Zhuang-zi. "I too would rather be dragging my tail in the mud." And he kept on fishing, without any further discussion.

Zhuang-zi had an old friend named Hui-zi. The two had different views on things, so often had arguments. For a period of time, Hui-zi was selected by the King of the state of Liang to be Prime Minister and to be in charge of affairs of State. Finding this out, Zhuang-zi went over to see him in the state of Liang. For whatever reason, some

people began to cast aspersions on Zhuang-zi in the presence of Hui-zi,
saying that Zhuang-zi was coming to visit in order to usurp Hui-zi's position. Since Hui-zi was afraid of losing this position, he actually believed
the rumors and he ordered his troops to find Zhuang-zi and arrest him.
They searched for three days and three nights, unsuccessfully. In fact,
Zhuang-zi was still on the road. He had heard about the planned arrest but
not changed his course at all, he simply kept heading towards the capital
of Liang.

When the two met, Zhuang-zi said to Hui-zi, "Are you familiar
with the bird in the south that is called the yuan chu? It flies from the
southern oceans to the northern seas, and it only stops to rest if it finds
a buttonwood tree. It only eats if it finds the fruit of bamboo, and it
only drinks from clear springs. Once it was flying over a particular
place where an owl had found a rotten, dead mouse. Seeing the yuan
chu fly overhead, the owl was afraid it might come down and try to
snatch its rotten mouse. So it raised its head and made very unpleasant
noises at the yuan chu. Is it because of your state of Liang that you are
now making similar noises at me?"

Hui-zi was mortified. He realized he had misunderstood Zhuang-
zi's intent. The two men restored their friendship and Zhuang-zi soon
returned to his woods, to continue his life as a hermit.

八岁咏诗的北朝名士祖莹

原文：

yíng bā suì　　 néng yǒng shī
莹 八 岁， 能 咏 诗；

mì qī suì　　 néng fù qí
泌 七 岁， 能 赋 棋。

bǐ yǐng wù　　 rén chēng qí
彼 颖 悟， 人 称 奇；

ěr yòu xué　　 dāng xiào zhī
尔 幼 学， 当 效 之。

故事：

　　南北朝（420—589）是中国历史上的一段长期分裂的时期。当时南朝文化水平比较高，北朝是由游牧民族建立的，开始的时候文化水平不高，经常因此而被南朝人嘲笑。然而就在这时候，北朝却出了一个酷爱读书的文化神童祖莹。

　　祖莹很小的时候就学会了识字看书，到八岁的时候，已能够背诵《诗经》《尚书》等传统文化典籍。十二岁时，他进了国家办的学校，学习更加刻苦。他特别喜欢读书，晚上

也不愿意放下书卷。父母担心这样下去他会生病，就禁止他晚上看书，但是这也不能够阻止祖莹。他偷偷藏好灯火，把父母派来看护他的仆人赶出房间；等父母睡觉之后，才重新点起灯来读书。他用衣服遮住窗户，以免家人看见灯光而来劝阻。

　　他爱好学习的事情在亲友之间到处传闻，大家都称他是

天才儿童。他还特别喜欢写文章，校长每次看了他的文章，都要感叹说："这个孩子的才能很突出，大多数学生都不可能达到他这样的水平，他以后会前程远大。"

这天，学校一位老师要听学生讲述对《尚书》的理解，学生们都按时赶到课堂。祖莹从夜里一直读书到天亮，上课时间快到了，才急急忙忙带着讲稿赶到。但他坐下一看，手里拿的并不是《尚书》讲稿，而是错拿了室友的另一门课的讲稿。这位老师性情严厉，祖莹不敢再回去取自己的讲稿，只好把拿错的讲稿放在面前，假装照着讲稿诵读，实际上是凭自己的记忆背诵了好几篇《尚书》，没有遗漏一个字。老师和同学们居然都没有发现他拿错讲稿，只有那位室友知道实情，告诉了老师，这下子，整个学校都轰动了。

当时北方的皇帝是北魏（386—534）孝文帝，他是一位杰出的少数民族政治家，鼓励本国人民学习汉族文化。他听说了祖莹的神奇表现，就召见这位神童，让他当面背诵儒家经典的内容，并且讲解其意义。祖莹表现出色，孝文帝大为欣赏。等祖莹出去之后，孝文帝对身边的大臣开玩笑说："听说上古时期，贤明的君主尧和舜把凶恶的罪臣共工流放到我们北方来，按说这里的人应该是共工的后代，怎么会出现祖莹这样的才子呢？"

祖莹受到皇帝的赏识而做了官，担任过很多职务，他渊博的学识和出众的文才经常受到人们赞赏。

Eight-year-old Zu Ying Recites Poetry in the Northern Dynasties

The Northern and Southern Dynasties period in China's history lasted from 420 to 589, and was characterized by fragmented political power. The level of culture in the South was regarded as higher than that in the North. The Northern Dynasties had been set up by nomadic tribes and, at the outset, had a lower standard of culture that was therefore often ridiculed by the South. It was just at this time that the Northern Dynasties produced a person of tremendous learning, famed for his genius even as a child.

As a small boy, Zu Ying learned to read and soon mastered the classics; by the age of eight, he could recite by heart such works as *The Book of Songs* (*Shi Jing*) and *the Shang Shu*. At the age of twelve, he entered a school administered by the State and began to study in earnest. He particularly loved to read, and would insist on reading into the night. His parents worried that he would get sick from so much reading, so they forbad him to read at night. Zu Ying would secretly store away a lantern and would chase away the servant appointed to keep watch; once his parents were asleep, he would light the lantern and start to read. He used his clothes to cover up the windows and hide

the light.

His love of learning spread far and wide and he began to be regarded as a child genius. He particularly liked to write compositions. The teacher would always exclaim upon reading one, "This child truly has a rare outstanding talent. This student has a bright future ahead of him."

One day, a teacher was asking students to explain their views of *the Shang Shu* to him. Students all arrived promptly at the study hall. Zu Ying had been reading all night long, until day broke, and he had to grab his manuscript and rush to make it on time. Once he got to class, he realized that he had brought the wrong paper, instead bringing the manuscript of a friend from a totally different class. This particular professor was very severe, so Zu Ying did not dare return home to find his own manuscript. When his turn came, he pretended to read from

the document in front of him, but in fact simply composed the speech off the top of his head. He was able correctly to recite many chapters of *the Shang Shu* from memory, without leaving out so much as one word. Professor and students had no idea he had brought the wrong manuscript, but the friend found out and informed everyone, after which the entire school congratulated him.

The Emperor in the North at the time was Xiao Wendi of the Northern Wei (386–534). He was an outstanding politician from a non-Chinese tribe, who encouraged his people to study the culture of the Han people (Chinese). He heard about Zu Ying's marvelous prowess, and called him in for an audience, asking him to recite classics of the Ru school of philosophy (Confucianism), as well as to explain what they meant. Zu Ying performed well and the Emperor was pleased. When he had gone out, Emperor Xiao Wendi turned to a senior official near him and said, "I've heard that the great sage emperors of antiquity, Yao and Shun, sent the evil minister Gong Gong into exile in the north back in ancient times. This person must be Gong Gong's descendant, otherwise how could such a talent as Zu Ying happen to be here?"

Zu Ying was asked by the Emperor to serve as an official and went on to serve in many responsible posts. His extensive knowledge and his outstanding cultural attainments were frequently lauded by the people.

蔡文姬辨琴与谢道韫咏雪

原文：

cài wén jī　　néng biàn qín
蔡 文 姬，　能 辨 琴；

xiè dào yùn　　néng yǒng yín
谢 道 韫，　能 咏 吟。

bǐ nǚ zǐ　　qiě cōng mǐn
彼 女 子，　且 聪 敏；

ěr nán zǐ　　dāng zì jǐng
尔 男 子，　当 自 警。

故事：

在中国古代，女性主要在家庭中做家务，受文化和艺术教育的机会很少。但即使是这样，仍然出现了一些在文化、艺术方面表现出杰出才能的女性。蔡文姬和谢道韫（yùn）就是其中两位。

蔡文姬生活在东汉末年。她的父亲蔡邕（yōng）是当时著名的文学家、书法家和音乐家。在父亲的熏陶下，蔡文姬从小就爱好文学和音乐，并表现出很好的天分。她六岁的时

候，有一天蔡邕在外面弹琴，她在自己的房间里听。听了一会儿，她忽然听出琴声传达出一种紧张的情绪，就跑出来看是怎么回事。原来，蔡邕正在弹琴，看见院子里面有一只猫在追捕老鼠，一个追，一个逃，他被这紧张的场面吸引住了，不知不觉表现在琴声中。

　　蔡邕发现女儿是个音乐天才，就有意考验她。有一次，他不小心弹断了一根琴弦，就问隔壁的女儿，断的是哪一根弦，文姬准确地告诉了他。蔡邕还想再考她一下，就故意又弹

断一根，结果女儿还是准确地判断了出来。蔡邕非常高兴，因为他的音乐艺术可以通过女儿传承下去了。

蔡邕死后，蔡文姬流落到北方匈奴地区，度过了很长时间的悲惨生活。后来曹操帮助她回到中原，她整理父亲的著作和藏书，还创作了不少诗歌和音乐作品。

谢道韫则是东晋时候的一位女诗人，从小就非常聪明，善于辩论。她的叔叔谢安高居宰相之位，与她谈话之后，称赞她拥有优秀诗人的修养。谢家是一个有名的大家族，有一次，天上下着大雪，谢安问聚集在一起的家族里的年轻人："你们说说，这雪可以比喻成什么？"有个男孩子答："就好像在天空中撒了很多盐。"谢道韫不以为然，说："雪花是轻飘飘的，盐粒则是沉甸甸的，哪里像呢？照我看，不如比喻成一团团的柳絮随着风飘飞起来。"听了这个优美的比喻，谢安等人都不禁鼓掌称赞。这个故事流传到后代，人们经常用"咏絮才"来形容女性出众的文学才华。

谢道韫长大后，嫁给了著名书法家王羲之的一个儿子。丈夫的才华不如谢道韫，但按当时的习惯，他可以跟客人们高谈阔论，而谢道韫只能躲在帘幕后面听。偶尔她也加入讨论，客人们无不惊叹她的见识和口才。

晚年的时候，谢道韫的丈夫死于战乱，她搬到了另一个地方居住。当地不少人，包括地方长官都向她请教各种问题，把她当成老师一样尊敬。

Cai Wenji Differentiates among the Strings of the Qin, and Xie Daoyun Extols the Snow

In ancient China, women mostly devoted themselves to house-work. Opportunities for cultural or artistic education were extremely few. Despite this, some outstanding women of high cultural and artistic attainment did appear from time to time. Cai Wenji and Xie Daoyun were two of them.

Cai Wenji lived in the latter years of the Eastern Han Dynasty. Her father, Cai Yong, was a famous man of letters at the time, as well as a calligrapher and a musician. Under his nurturing influence, Cai Wenji learned to love both literature and music from an early age, and displayed a natural aptitude for them. When she was six years old, one day Cai Yong was outdoors playing the qin while she was in her own room, listening. After listening a while, she heard a sudden surge of anxious emotion in the music and she ran outdoors to see what was going on. It turned out Cai Yong had been playing when he saw a cat stalking a mouse in the courtyard. The chasing and the pouncing had absorbed his attention and unwittingly been transmitted to the music.

Cai Yong discovered that his daughter had musical abilities and he began to test her. Once, he unintentionally broke a string, so he asked his daughter, who was next door, which string it had been. When she answered correctly, he tested her further and this time intentionally broke a string, and still she knew which one it had been. Cai Yong was glad because he felt that now his own musical art could be transmitted on down through his daughter.

After Cai Yong died, Cai Wenji wandered up to the northern area of the Hun where she spent a long and apparently tragic life. Cao Cao later helped her return to the central plains, where she organized her father's papers and his library. She also went on to compose a number of literary and musical creations.

Xie Daoyun was a female poet during the time of the Eastern Jin Dynasty. From childhood, she was precocious and loved disputation. Her uncle Xie An served on high as Prime Minister, and after talking to her he confirmed that she had a superior poet's level of sophistication. The Xie were a major clan; one day it snowed hard all day and night and Xie An gathered together all the young people in this clan. He asked them, "How would you describe this snow? What metaphor would you use?" One boy answered, "It's as though salt had been sprinkled throughout the sky." Xie Daoyun felt that was inappropriate. "Snowflakes are light and floating," she pointed out. "Grains of salt

are heavy. I see this snow as soft willow catkins floating through the air." This analogy delighted Xie An, and the story has come down in history in the way that people now describe an outstanding female literary talent as one who has the talent to appreciate catkins.

Xie Daoyun married one of the sons of the famous calligrapher Wang Xizhi when she grew up. Her husband was somewhat mediocre, but the custom at the time was for wives to stay in the background, out of sight, when guests came for a visit. Still, she joined in the discussion from time to time and guests were always amazed at her knowledge and verbal abilities.

In her later years, Xie Daoyun's husband died in the midst of warfare and turmoil and she herself moved to another place to live. The local people in that place, including the local officials, always asked for her advice on various issues and accorded her the respect of a great teacher.

神童刘晏

原文:

táng liú yàn　　fāng qī suì
唐刘晏，　方七岁，

jǔ shén tóng　　zuò zhèng zì
举神童，　作正字。

bǐ suī yòu　　shēn yǐ shì
彼虽幼，　身已仕；

ěr yòu xué　　miǎn ér zhì
尔幼学，　勉而致。

故事:

　　唐朝（618—907）是中国历史上最强盛的朝代，在唐玄宗的时候，唐朝的各项事业达到了顶峰。有一年，为了表示庆祝，请求上天继续保佑大唐帝国，唐玄宗跑到泰山去举行祭祀活动。

　　祭祀结束之后，唐玄宗会见当地的官员和名人。这时候，一个小孩也赶来，声称要把一篇文章献给皇帝。唐玄宗听说这孩子只有七岁，有点儿好奇，就让他到自己面前来读

那篇文章。这个孩子叫刘晏，在当地早就被人们称为神童。面对皇帝，他一点儿也不紧张，大声念了自己写的称颂这次祭祀活动的文章。以他的年龄而论，这篇文章已经写得很好了。唐玄宗又问了他几个别的问题，小刘晏也对流如流。唐玄宗于是授给他一个官职，命令他去校对和抄写宫廷的藏书。七岁的孩子因为献给皇帝文章而被授予官职，这件事很快传扬开来，许多人都想认识这位神童。因为年龄太小，刘

晏的官服和帽子都是特制的，人们看他穿着官服的样子，都觉得很有意思。

小刘晏追随在唐玄宗身边，唐玄宗认为他还是个孩子，有时会问他一些有趣的问题来开玩笑。可是刘晏经过认真思考，都能将话题转换到严肃而深刻的方面。后来，唐玄宗就不敢再把他当小孩子看待了。

长大之后，刘晏开始担任一些管理地方和中央政府具体事务的官职，积累了丰富的经验，尤其是在管理经济方面，更表现出杰出的才干。到唐玄宗的儿子唐肃宗时，他被调到京城长安，开始主管整个帝国的财政。当时唐王朝经过多年战乱，经济萧条，刘晏采取了一系列有效的改革措施，使唐王朝的经济得到了恢复和发展，国库又渐逐充实起来。

管理这个庞大帝国的财政，是一件很艰巨的工作。作为一位杰出的理财家，刘晏选用人才的标准是精明能干、忠于职守、廉洁奉公，他指挥的庞大经济系统因此而运转顺利。

但是最后，一位性情暴躁、刚愎自用的皇帝上台了，他听信谗言，认为刘晏犯下一些罪行，下令杀死了刘晏。政府派人去检查刘晏的家，发现他家里连女仆都没有，他死后留下的家庭财产不过是两车书籍和数量很少的粮食。一位杰出的理财专家和正直的官员，就这样含冤而死了，人们都非常惋惜。

Child Prodigy Liu Yan

The Tang dynasty (618–907) was the most powerful in China's history. It reached its height in a number of different aspects during the reign of Emperor Tang Xuanzong. One year, in order to express appreciation and to ask Heaven to continue to protect imperial Tang, Tang Xuanzong went over to Taishan (Mount Tai) to conduct offering ceremonies and rituals.

After the rituals were completed, the Emperor held an audience with the local officials and famous people. A young boy came up at that time and declared that he wished to dedicate a composition he had written to the Emperor. Tang Xuanzong heard that this child was only seven years old and, curious, he asked the boy to read the composition to him in person. This child was called Liu Yan, and he had long been recognized in the region as a kind of child prodigy. He was not at all afraid in the presence of the Emperor but read out his composition in a loud voice, extolling the offerings and rituals. For his age, the composition was not too bad. Tang Xuanzong then asked him various questions and Liu Yan answered them fluently. Tang Xuanzong then bestowed an official rank upon the child, and ordered him to compare

and copy out the books in the court library. For a seven-year-old to be made an official by the government was news that soon travelled throughout the land and many people wanted to meet this prodigy. Due to his age, the usual official's robes would not fit Liu Yan, so special ones were made for him so that he could carry out his duties.

Little Liu Yan often accompanied the Emperor, who looked upon him as still a child and who would make jokes about various things, thinking that this would amuse him. Instead, Liu Yan always took the subject very seriously and found a way to turn the conversation into something of substance. As a result, Tang Xuanzong no longer dared to treat the boy as merely a child.

After getting older, Liu Yan began to assume official positions that put him in charge of both regional and central governmental affairs. He accumulated a wealth of experience, especially in terms of economic management where his outstanding talents were put to best

use. When Tang Xuanzong's son became Emperor, Tang Suzong, Liu Yan was sent to the capital city of Chang'an to be in charge of the entire financial affairs of the Tang empire. The Tang Dynasty had been through many years of warfare at the time and its finances were in bad shape, but Liu Yan adopted a series of reform measures that were effective, allowing the Tang dynasty to restore growth and gradually fill the State treasury again.

Managing the finances of such a huge empire was an enormous task. As an outstanding manager of financial affairs, Liu Yan's standard for choosing deputies was highly astute. They had to be intelligent and capable, but also faithful in the discharge of their duties, as well as honest. As a result, the enormous economic system that he administered was able to operate smoothly.

In the end, however, an emperor assumed the throne who was cruel and opinionated and who was taken in by slanderous rumors. He thought that Liu Yan had committed certain crimes and so he had him put to death. When the government sent people to investigate the situation at his household, they found that instead of amassing wealth he lived an extremely simple life. His household possessions included two boxes of books and an insignificant amount of grain. For an outstanding financial wizard and an upright official to die in such a wrongful way has always been thought of as highly regrettable.

Legendary Tales
传说故事

伏羲发明八卦

原文：

zì xī nóng　　zhì huáng dì

自羲农，至黄帝，

hào sān huáng　　jū shàng shì

号三皇，居上世。

故事：

在中国的神话传说中，伏羲（xī）是远古时代的一位君主。据说他的母亲到野外去玩耍，看见一个巨大的脚印，就好奇地用脚试着踩了踩，结果就怀了孕。她生下一个儿子，就是伏羲。原来这个脚印是神留下的，所以伏羲长得跟那位神一样，人头而蛇身，并且具有非凡的神力。

伏羲和女神女娲（wā）被认为是婚姻之神和人类始祖。传说伏羲和女娲是兄妹，他们在湖中捞鱼，有一只巨大的白色乌龟游过来说："一百天之后将发生大灾难，我是来救你们的，请每天送我一条鱼。"兄妹俩就每天给白龟送鱼。一百天后，果然天塌地陷，发生了大洪水。伏羲兄妹在白龟的帮助下躲过了灾难。洪水消退之后，世界上已经没有其他人了，于是兄妹俩按照天神的旨意结合，繁衍人类，成为人类的始祖。后来人们把伏羲、女娲的形象刻画在祖先的坟墓和纪念祖先的祠庙里，希望他们保佑他们所繁衍的人类后代。

相传伏羲有很多文化发明，比如鱼网和预知未来的八卦。

远古时代，人们用手来捉鱼，捕获的数量很少。有一天，伏羲看到蜘蛛结网捉虫子，受到启发，他将绳子编成网，用来捉鱼。从此之后，人们就能捕获大量的鱼，拥有了

足够的食物。

八卦是伏羲最重要的发明，它是中国古代预测未来的工具。据说，由于伏羲是一位道德高尚的君主，所以天神派遣了一匹龙马出现在黄河里。这匹龙马背上有神秘的图案，伏羲仔细观察这些图案之后，发明了八种基本符号，即八卦，分别用来象征天、地、水、火、雷、风、山、泽等自然界的事物。通过这八种基本符号的组合，概括宇宙万物，从而预知事物在未来的发展变化。八卦后来演变成六十四卦，最终发展为中国古典哲学的重要典籍《易经》。

还有一些传说认为，伏羲死后成为东方天帝，负责管理东方的天空和春天。

Fu Xi Invents the "Ba Gua"

According to myths and legends, Fu Xi was a monarch in ancient times. It is said that his mother went out walking one day and saw an enormous footprint. Curious, she put her foot in this footprint and the result was that she became pregnant. She bore a son, who was Fu Xi. It turned out this footprint had been left by a god who Fu Xi grew up to resemble: he had the head of a man and the snake of a body, and he had extraordinary godlike strength.

Fu Xi and Nü Wa are considered the gods of marriage and also the progenitors of all mankind. Legend has it that the two were brother and sister, and that they were out hauling fish from a lake one day when a huge white tortoise swam by and said, "In one hundred days, there is going to be a major disaster. I am here to save you. Please send me a fish every day for the next hundred days." The two accordingly gave the tortoise a fish every day and, one hundred days later, the skies and earth did indeed turn upside down and a tremendous flood came over the land. Fu Xi and his little sister were rescued by the tortoise and avoided disaster. When the flood waters receded, nobody else existed on earth but the two of them. As a result, the two, as accord-

ing to the will of heaven, joined in union and the result was the fertile increase in human kind. They became the start of human beings. Later, people carved images of Fu Xi and Nü Wa into their ancestors' graves and temples that were built to memorialize their ancestors. They hoped that the two would protect and help multiply their own descendants.

It is said that Fu Xi invented a number of things that advanced human culture, such as fishing nets and also Ba Gua.

In the most ancient times, people used their hands to catch fish. One day, Fu Xi saw how spiders use the spiderweb to catch insects and this gave him the idea of using a similar net to catch fish. He made the first one out of ropes. After this invention, people could catch many more fish and began to have enough to eat.

The Ba Gua was Fu Xi's most important invention. It was used to foretell the future in ancient times in China. It is said that since Fu Xi was an ethical and upstanding monarch, heaven sent him a "dragon horse" which appeared in the Yellow River. This dragon horse had mysterious patterns on its back. Fu Xi examined these carefully and invented the system of Ba Gua symbols as a result. They could be used to symbolize heaven, earth, water, fire, thunder, wind, mountains, marshes, and all the many natural phenomena in the world. Through combining the basic Ba Gua symbols, one could cover all the multitude of things in the universe and thereby foretell what was going to happen, both the future development of and the changes in all things. Eventually, the Ba Gua (Eight Gua) evolved into Sixty-four Gua, and in the end they formed the basis of *The Book of Changes*, *the Yi Jing*, an important classic in ancient Chinese philosophy.

Other legends say that after Fu Xi died he became the heavenly king of the East, responsible for governing all of the East's heavens, as well as its springtime.

神农的传说

原文：

zì xī nóng   zhì huáng dì
自 羲 农 ， 至 黄 帝 ，

hào sān huáng   jū shàng shì
号 三 皇 ， 居 上 世 。

故事：

中国人自称"炎黄子孙"，炎就是炎帝，黄就是黄帝，他们分别是上古时代两个强大部落的首领。炎帝又叫神农，相传他发明了农业生产和医药，因此成为农业神和医药之神。

据说，神农的母亲是一位国王的妃子，因为受到一条龙的感应而怀孕，生下一个孩子，长着牛头和人身，他就是后来的炎帝神农。神农诞生的时候，地上自动出现九口水井，井水彼此相连。牛和井水的征兆，预示着这个孩子将带给人类农业技术。

上古的时候，人类吃的都是野生的植物、动物，经常生

病。神农看到这样的情景，很不忍心，便祈求天神改善人们的生活。天神受到感动，下了一场五谷雨，把各种粮食的种子送到人间。神农收集起这些种子，分别播种到合适的土地里。为了播种和收割这些粮食，他还发明冶炼金属的技术，造出斧子，又用斧子砍削木头，制造出各种农业工具。在他的教导下，人们逐渐把荒野开辟为良田，并一步步掌握了农业生产技术。

据说神农神通广大，向天神祈求，想要雨，就下雨；想要晴天，就变成晴天。在他的治理下，中国的大地上五谷丰收，人类的食物充裕，再也不会饿肚子了。这样，神农就成了农业之神。因为发明了农业，炎帝神农至今仍受到人们的祭祀。

那个时候，人类还饱受各种疾病之苦，经常有人因为生病而悲惨地死去。神农决心找到治病救人的方法。他冒险去尝试各种植物的药性，据说他的身体是透明的，吃了某种植物之后，可以看到植物在他肚子里的反应。通过这种方法，他确定了很多种草药的治疗效果。但他因为尝试的植物太多，经常中毒，有时候一天之内竟几十次中毒。幸亏他具有神性，才不至于死亡。后来，他获得了一根神奇的红色鞭子，无论什么植物，只要用这根鞭子一抽，立刻就能够向他显示出它的性质。神农根据植物的不同性质，治疗人类的各种疾病。他将这些经验总结成一本书，即中国第一本药学著作《本草》。因

此，神农又被人们尊为医药之神。

据说在炎帝神农治理天下的大部分时间，男人耕种，女人织布，没有盗窃，更没有抢劫和战争，人们过着幸福安宁的生活。但到了炎帝时代末期，社会道德开始衰败，一些部落开始相互侵略，抢夺土地、财物和人口。后来，强大的黄帝部落战胜了炎帝部落，重新恢复了和平。这两大部落，就是今天中国人的祖先。

至于炎帝本人，一种说法是他最后被黄帝杀掉了，另一种说法是他逃到了南方，成为南方天帝，负责管理南方的天空和夏天。

The Legend of Shen Nong, the God of Agriculture

Chinese call themselves the grandsons of Yan Huang. Yan refers to Yan Di, or Emperor Yan. Huang refers to Huang Di, or Emperor Huang. Each of these two was the head of a powerful tribe in ancient times. Yan Di is also known as Shen Nong, which means literally "the god of agriculture." Legend has it that he invented the practice of agriculture and also pharmacology, and thereby became the god of agriculture as well as the god of medicine.

It is said that the mother of Shen Nong was the concubine of a King. Influenced by "response received from a Loong," she became pregnant and bore a child. It had the head of a water buffalo and the body of a man, and this child later became Yan Di Shen Nong. When Shen Nong was born, nine wells spontaneously appeared on the earth, the waters of which were all interconnected. The water buffalo and the omen of the springs foretold that this child would be bringing the technology of agriculture to mankind.

People in the earliest times ate things raw, such as all plants and animals, and as a result they often fell sick. Shen Nong looked over this situation and began to ask the heavens to improve people's lives.

The gods of the heavens were moved by this, and they sent down a rain of five grains (many grains), by so doing giving seeds of all the various grains to humans. Shen Nong collected these and planted them in different and appropriate places. In order to sow and also to reap the grain, he then invented metallurgy. He created axes, and used the axes to fell trees; he manufactured all kinds of agricultural tools. Under his guidance, people gradually turned wastelands into fertile fields, and step by step mastered technologies for agricultural production.

It is said that Shen Nong had a close tie to the gods. If he asked the heavens for rain, then it rained. If he asked for a clear day, it was clear. Under his administration, harvests were abundant on China's vast land and mankind had enough to eat. They no longer had to go hungry. As a result, Shen Nong became the god of agriculture and, to this day, people in China pay homage to Yan Di Shen Nong by sending him offerings.

Back then, mankind also suffered from all kinds of illnesses, and people died premature and grievous deaths due to getting sick. Shen Nong decided that he would find methods to treat people and save them. He took the risk of trying out the medicinal value of various kinds of plants on himself—it is said that his body was transparent, and he could see where the reaction was inside himself to any given substance. Through these methods, he ascertained the efficacy of all

kinds of herbaceous medicines. Since he tried too many plants on himself, however, he was often sick; within one day he might suffer dozens of attacks of different illnesses. Fortunately, he was empowered with "godness" and did not actually die as a result. Later, he acquired

a mysterious and marvelous red whip. All he had to do was snap any plant with his whip and it would instantly reveal its nature to him. Shen Nong was thereby able to treat the different illnesses of mankind according to the different natures of plants. He put together the results in a book called *Ben Cao*, translated into English as *Chinese Materia Medica*. This was China's first work of pharmacology and, as a result, Shen Nong is also regarded as the god of medicine in China.

For most of the time "all under heaven" was being governed by Yan Di Shen Nong, all was in its proper place. Men tilled the fields, women wove cloth, there were no robbers and certainly no plundering and warfare. People lived peaceful and fortunate lives. Towards the end of the Yan Di period, however, social ethics began to break down. Some tribes began to invade the territory of others, taking land, goods, and people. Later, the powerful Huang Di tribe defeated the Yan Di tribe and again restored peace to the land. These two tribes are therefore the ancestors of today's Chinese people.

As for what happened to Yan Di, one theory has it that he was killed in the end by Huang Di. Another says that he escaped to the South, where he became the Heavenly King of the South, responsible for governing the heavens of the south and also its summertime.

黄帝和蚩尤的大战

原文：

zì xī nóng   zhì huáng dì
自羲农，至黄帝，

hào sān huáng   jū shàng shì
号三皇，居上世。

故事：

　　被视为中华民族祖先的黄帝，也是一位远古帝王。他通过战争，击败了炎帝神农和蚩（chī）尤两个强大的对手，最终登上昆仑山最高神殿的宝座，成为中国神话中最高的神。黄帝和他的下属们还贡献了很多文化发明。

　　相传黄帝的母亲受到闪电感应，怀孕二十五个月之后才生下黄帝。黄帝是一个雷雨神，他长着四张脸，可以同时监视四方的情况。同时他还掌握着宇宙间最强大的力量——雷电。

　　黄帝面临的是一个战乱年代。他组织起强大的军队，先是与炎帝进行了一场大战。炎帝使用火攻击黄帝，黄帝则依靠雷雨抵抗。随后，黄帝率领老虎、豹子、狼、熊、老鹰等动物

组成的军队发动攻击，经过三次交锋，彻底击败炎帝，取得了最高统治权。

但不久，另一个强大部落的首领蚩尤又发动了叛乱。蚩尤是一个恶神，头上长着坚硬锋利的角，耳朵上的毛发也都像刀锋一样。他有八十一个铜头铁额的兄弟，生性凶猛，能够吃沙子和石头。蚩尤又发明了很多兵器，包括长矛、弓箭、战斧、盾牌等，经常攻击其他部族的人民。他率领自己的兄弟们，又发动了山林水泽之中的各种鬼怪，加上很多军队，向黄帝发起进攻。黄帝也率领各种神灵和数量众多的军队前来迎战。

蚩尤精通阵法，还能呼风唤雨，喷烟吐雾。他带来一场大雾，把黄帝及其部下包围在里面，使他们分不清东西南北，结果蚩尤九战九胜。幸亏黄帝有一个部下利用磁铁发明了指南车，就是在车子上设立一个用磁铁造的仙人像，不论车子怎么旋转，仙人像的手指永远指向南方。在指南车的指引下，黄帝的军队总算突围出来了。

蚩尤又请来风神和雨神，发动了一场狂风暴雨，把黄帝一方冲击得四散奔逃。黄帝只好到天上，请求女神女魃（bá）的帮助。女魃长得很难看，头是秃的，但她的秃头发出光芒，驱散狂风骤雨，让人间烈日高照，把地面上的雨水都晒干了。黄帝一方趁机大举进攻，将蚩尤一方彻底打败。

蚩尤也被活捉，押解到黄帝面前。黄帝将蚩尤处死。蚩尤被杀之后，他身上带的木枷都被血液染红了。人们把这木枷抛弃到荒野上，它立刻变成一片枫树林，每一片叶子都鲜红如血。

黄帝一方举行了盛大的庆祝活动，黄帝和众神尽情享受胜利的喜悦。宇宙秩序重新恢复，和平重返人间。虽然以后又发生了一些反叛活动，但都没有成功。黄帝和他的部下发明了房子、锅、服装、车子和文字，引导人类开始了一个崭新的时代。

The Great War between Huang Di and Chi You

The being who is regarded as the ancestor of the nation of Chinese people was also a monarch or emperor in ancient times. Through means of force, he attacked and defeated two major opponents, namely Yan Di Shen Nong and Chi You. In the end, he assumed the highest throne in the Kunlun Mountain palaces of the gods and became the supreme god in Chinese mythology. Huang Di and his various associates also contributed much in the way of cultural inventions to mankind.

It is said that Huang Di's mother, responding to a force of lightning, conceived a child and twenty-five months later gave birth to Huang Di. Huang Di is a god of rain and thunder. He has four faces and therefore can see what is happening in four different directions at the same time. He holds the greatest force of the universe in his hands, thunder and lightning.

Huang Di came into the world when it was confronting an era of warfare and chaos. He assembled a large army and first went to war against Yan Di. Yan Di used fire to attack Huang Di, and Huang Di used rain and lightning to resist the attack. After that, he led a united army of tigers, leopards, wolves, bears, and eagles in an all-out charge.

After clashing in battle three times, he totally defeated Yan Di and won ultimate governing power.

Not long after, however, another powerful tribe led by Chi You mobilized revolt. Chi You was an evil god, with hard sharp horns on his head, and with ears that sprouted out hair like daggers. He had

eighty-one brothers with copper heads and iron foreheads. They were all "ferocious" in nature and could eat sand and stones. Chi You also invented a number of weapons including long spears, bow and arrow, battle axes, shields and so on, and he often used these in invading neighboring tribes. He stood at the front of his own brothers and also mobilized the evil spirits of the woods and marshes, in addition to his own armies, in order to begin the attack on Huang Di. Huang Di also led all kinds of spirits on his side, as well as countless troops in the charge to meet the oncoming foe.

Chi You excelled in the art of arraying battle forces, and could call forth wind and rain, smoke and mist. He now called a great fog down upon the land that enveloped Huang Di and his troops, so that they were unable to distinguish north from south, east from west. As a result, Chi You was successful in winning nine battles out of nine engagements. Fortunately, one of Huang Di's subordinates invented the south-facing chariot, using magnetism. A magnetic image of an immortal being was placed in the chariot, and no matter which direction you turned the chariot, the immortal would also face towards the south. With guidance from this south-facing chariot, Huang Di's army was able to break out of the encirclement.

Chi You then asked the gods of wind and of rain to mobilize a tremendously wild storm, that would pummel Huang Di into scattering

in all directions. There was nothing Huang Di could do then, but go up to heaven and ask the female god Nü Ba for her help. Nü Ba was extremely ugly. Her head was bald, but it shone forth with a kind of light that could dispel all stormy weather and allow fierce sunshine to shine down from on high. This light dried up all the rainwater on the ground. Huang Di seized the opportunity and attacked, and this time triumphed over Chi You.

Chi You was taken alive. He was forced into the presence of Huang Di, where Huang Di had him put to death. After Chi You was killed, it was noticed that the wooden shackles on his body had been dyed a deep red. People took these shackles out to the wastelands and scattered their pieces, whereupon they instantly turned into a forest of maple trees, each leaf the color of fresh red blood.

Huang Di then organized a great victory celebration. He and the assembled gods tasted the satisfaction of triumphing over evil. Order had been restored in the universe, peace had returned to mankind. Although some disturbances and troubles were to occur later, these were not successful. Huang Di and his troops invented housing, cooking pots, clothing, vehicles, the writing of scripts and so on, and led mankind forth into a new era.

尧舜禅让

原文：

táng yǒu yú hào èr dì
唐 有 虞 ， 号 二 帝 ，

xiāng yī xùn chēng shèng shì
相 揖 逊 ， 称 盛 世 。

故事：

相传在上古时候，中国的帝王不将王位传给自己的儿子，而是经过考察和选拔，将王位让给德才兼备的继承人，这种方式叫做禅（shàn）让。尧将王位禅让给舜、舜又将王位禅让给禹的故事，一直被人们传诵。

尧帝是远古时代道德高尚的圣人和伟大的帝王。他生活极其简朴，王宫和平民住的茅草屋差不多，饮食、衣服、用具都很简陋。但他从不忘记引导和爱护人民的职责。他听说有人饿肚子，就责备自己："是我使他吃不上饭。"有人犯罪，他就责备自己没有管理好："是我害了他。"由于工作繁忙，尧帝的身躯瘦得和风干的肉一样。他高尚的品德深深

感动了人民，尽管遇到严重的旱灾、大洪水等灾难，但是人民仍然坚决追随他。

尧帝选择一些品德高尚、才能卓著的人做大臣，让他们协助自己治理国家。在他们的共同努力下，国家繁荣富强，人民生活富裕，劳动之余，还有很多空闲时间，可以聚在一起做游戏。

这一天，有位年过八十的老翁和大家一起快乐地玩扔木片的游戏，有人感慨说："这都是尧帝的功劳呀，尧帝真伟大！"老翁很不以为然，说："太阳出来，我就开始干活；太阳落山，我就去休息。吃的粮食，是我自己种的；喝的水，是我自己打井挖出来的；穿的衣服，是我自己织的。请问，尧帝的功劳在哪里呢？"那人被问得哑口无言。老翁并不觉得尧帝有多么伟大，而这恰恰是尧所希望的。他不把国泰民安看作自己的功绩，而认为这是帝王应尽的职责。

尧帝认为，帝王的位子应该属于贤人。他发现自己的儿子不是合适的继承人，就主动将帝位禅让给舜帝。

在中国古人心目中，舜帝是一位道德楷模。舜的母亲很早就去世了，他的父亲叫瞽（gǔ）叟，意思是眼睛失明的老头。后来瞽叟再婚，与继妻又生下一个小儿子。舜对父亲和继母非常孝顺，对弟弟也总是尽力照顾，但瞽叟、继母和弟弟却想杀死舜。

一天，他们让舜去清理水井，舜下了井后，父母用大石

头堵住井口，要置他于死地。幸好，舜的孝心感动了上天，井下突然出现一条通道，通向邻居家的水井，舜因此而得救。

舜逃到别的地方去生活。在他的影响下，周围的人都变得善良谦让。舜成为一个众望所归的人。尧帝听说了舜的事

迹，将他找来，在确认了他的品行和能力之后，把自己的两个女儿嫁给他。

舜带着两个妻子返回家乡，和她们一起照顾父母。瞽叟、继母他们仍然想加害于舜。舜对妻子们说："父母的话，我应该听从。可是，万一出了事，他们的名誉会受损害。怎样才能避免发生这种事情呢？"妻子们便取出一件画着飞鸟图案的衣服给舜穿上。舜爬上高高的谷仓清扫灰尘，瞽叟和小儿子却在下面放火，想烧死他。舜穿着那件衣服，安全地落在地上。事后，他像往常一样对待父母。

最终，舜通过了各种考验，从尧帝那儿继承了王位。他的努力也使瞽叟、继母、弟弟受到感动，一家人从此和好。

舜帝委派大禹治理洪水。大禹走遍全国，经历千辛万苦，成功治理了包括黄河、淮河在内的所有河流。晚年，舜帝把王位禅让给大禹。

大禹死后，他的儿子启继承了王位。启不再实行禅让制，而是将王位传给自己的儿子，于是创立了中国历史上第一个王朝——夏（前2070—前1600）。

Yao and Shun Practice Succession by Merit

It is said that, in ancient days in China, monarchs passed the kingship on to those with merit and not to their sons. The successor had to undergo testing and selection, and had to come up to ethical standards as well as those of talent. This kind of succession was known by a special term that meant "succession by merit." Yao passed the kingship on in this manner to Shun, and Shun in turn passed it on to Yu. This has always been what people said.

The sovereign named Yao was a man of supremely high ethical standards, a kind of great sage as well as a monarch. He lived in a supremely simple fashion, his palace being not much better than the thatched huts of common people, his food, clothing and utensils similarly plain. He never lost sight of his obligation to guide the people and to love and protect them. When he heard that someone was hungry, he felt it was his fault, "I am the one who made it hard for him to get a meal." When he heard that someone had committed a crime, he said, "I am the one who harmed him." Due to the pressures of work, Yao's body was as thin as a strip of dried jerky. His moral bearing profoundly affected people, who resolutely supported and followed him

despite any kind of natural disaster such as floods or drought.

Yao selected men of outstanding moral character and talent to assist him as senior officials, and to help him in the task of administering the country. Under their united efforts, the country was prosperous and strong, people's lives were fortunate, in addition to work there was time to relax and people could get together to play a little.

One day, an old fellow over eighty years old was playing at tossing wooden chips with some friends and someone happened to say, "All of this leisure is due to the hard work of our monarch Yao. He is certainly a great sovereign!" The old man felt differently. He replied, "The sun gets up, I go to work. The sun goes down behind the mountain, I come home to rest. The grain I eat I planted myself. The water I drink is from the well I dug. The clothes I wear I wove myself. I ask you, what

does Sovereign Yao have to do with any of this?" The people listening were speechless. That the old man did not think Yao was so great was, in fact, precisely what Yao wanted. He did not look on the glory of the country and the security of the people as a great act but rather simply as the natural obligation of a ruler.

The monarch Yao felt that the position of head of a dynasty should belong to a "virtuous man." He discovered that his own son was not appropriate in this regard, so he voluntarily passed the kingship on to Shun.

In the minds of people long ago in China, Shun was the very model of ethical behavior. Shun's mother died when he was young and his father, called Gu Sou, which means an old man who has lost his sight, remarried and husband and wife had another son. Yao was very filial to his father as well as to the step-mother and her son, but his little half-brother, his father, and his step-mother had plans to kill him.

One day, they had Shun clean out the well. He went down inside, and the father and stepmother immediately placed a large stone on top, blocking it up, trying to seal him into his "death place." Fortunately, Shun's good heart moved the heavens above and a connection to the neighboring well suddenly appeared underground. Shun was able to emerge from the neighboring well unscathed.

After that, Shun fled to another place to live. Under his influence,

the people around him all became kind-hearted and good to one another. The monarch Yao now heard about this man Shun and called him in to confirm his merits and his talents. After that, he gave his two daughters to Shun in marriage.

With his two wives, Shun returned to his homeland and, together they looked after the old father and step-mother although both of these still wanted to hurt Shun. Shun said to his wives, "I must obey my parents' words. However, if something were to happen to me, their reputations would suffer. How can I prevent that from happening?" The wives drew forth a piece of clothing that had a flying bird painted on it and gave it to Shun. Shun climbed up on the tall granary to sweep the dust from it, while below the old man and his little son were preparing to light a fire, thinking to burn him to death. Putting on the piece of clothing, Shun was able to float safely down to the ground. After this, he continued to treat his parents in the same filial manner.

In the end, after passing all kinds of tests of his mettle, Shun received the succession of the throne from Yao. He also continued to try to improve his relations with Gu Sou, the second wife, and the little half-brother, and in the end they were moved by his efforts and all were reconciled.

The monarch Shun then sent the Great Yu to calm the flood waters. Great Yu went throughout the country, enduring a myriad of hardships,

but succeeded in controlled the flooding of all the rivers, including the Yellow River and the Huai River. In his later years, Shun passed the kingship on to Yu, in this same manner of succession through merit.

After the Great Yu died, his son took over the kingship. No longer following the practice of succession by merit, the kingship now started to be passed from king to son. In this manner, the first dynasty in China's history came to be established, that of the Xia (2070–1600 BCE).

Historical Tales
历史故事

武王伐纣

原文：

zhōu wǔ wáng   shǐ zhū zhòu
周 武 王，始 诛 纣，

bā bǎi zǎi   zuì cháng jiǔ
八 百 载，最 长 久。

故事：

　　商朝（前1600—前1046）最后一个帝王叫纣（zhòu），他刚登上帝王之位时，还是很有作为的，与东方的部落作战，取得了一系列胜利。但渐渐地，他变得骄横（hèng）起来，贪图享乐。他下令扩建都城，修造了华丽的宫殿和花园，过着穷奢极欲的生活：吃饭用的筷子是用象牙做的，酒杯则是玉做的；酒倾倒在一个大池子里，悬挂起来的肉看上去像一片树林；要求各个地方献美女，对宠爱的美女，他言听计从，答应她们的一切不合理要求。

　　为了维持自己的享乐生活，纣王向人民征收很重的赋税，人民对他越来越不满。人们起来反抗，纣王就以酷刑来镇压。他发明了一种叫"炮烙"的酷刑，把铜柱放在火上烧红，强迫"犯人"在铜柱上行走，"犯人"站立不住，就掉到火里烧死。大臣们规劝他，他或者不理会，或者将其处死。他

的叔叔比干规劝他，他竟残忍地挖出了比干的心。他的哥哥则逃走了。就这样，商纣王变成了中国历史上有名的暴君。

与此同时，商的属国周则强大起来。周本来是个小国，在现在的陕西省。周文王死后，他的儿子周武王继承王位。武王看到商纣王如此荒淫无道，就准备讨伐商纣。在姜尚、周公旦等人的辅佐和帮助下，周国实行有利于人民的制度，变得日益强大。

后来，周武王看到时机成熟了，就率领几万精锐部队向商的都城进发。一路上，他联合了许多同样对商纣王的统治不满的部族，队伍更加庞大。周武王向人们指出纣王的各种罪恶，动员大家一起推翻其统治。这支联军很快推进到了距离商的都城不远的一个叫牧野的地方（在现在的河南省淇县）。

当时商朝的军队主力远在东方作战，无法赶回来，纣王没有办法，只好将大批奴隶临时武装起来，命令他们到牧野与周军决战。但这些奴隶连饭都吃不饱，怎么能有战斗力呢？况且他们很恨纣王，于是，奴隶大军就投降了周武王，反过来帮助周军进攻纣王。纣王逃到宫中高高的楼台上，无路可退，只好放火自杀了。也有人说，他是被周武王抓住处死了。

商朝就这样灭亡了，周武王建立的周朝（前1046—前256）成为中国历史上存在时间最长的王朝。

King Wu Attacks King Zhou

The last emperor in the Shang Dynasty (1600–1046 BCE) was named Zhou. For a period of time after assuming the throne, he ruled in a capable and responsible manner, winning a series of conquests against tribes in the east. In time, however, he became cruel, arrogant, greedy, and self-indulgent. Upon his orders, a capital city was built that was full of palaces and gardens, where he led a dissolute life. He had a large pond filled with wine, and the meat hanging in his storage rooms to dry looked like a forest. He commanded various regions of his domain to send him beautiful women, and he did whatever his favorite concubines asked him to do.

In order to maintain this luxurious life, King Zhou inflicted heavy taxes on the populace, who became more and more dissatisfied with his rule. When revolts began, King Zhou dealt with them severely through cruel punishments. He invented a kind of torture in which a copper beam was set over a burning fire, on which an 'offender' had to walk back and forth. As the fire heated the copper, it scorched the feet of the person who eventually fell into the fire and burned to death. Senior officials admonished King Zhou to change his ways, but he either

disregarded them or had them executed. His uncle Bi Gan also tried to discipline him, upon which King Zhou had Bi Gan's heart torn out. His own brother fled. King Zhou became one of the infamous tyrants in Chinese history.

While all this was taking place, the state of Chou, a subject state to Shang, was growing ever more powerful. A small country at the beginning, it was located in the current position of Shaanxi Province. After the King Wen of Chou died, his son succeeded to the throne, a man called Chou Wuwang, or King Wu of Chou. King Wu could see that King Zhou of the state of Shang was ruling in a chaotic manner and he decided to plan for an invasion. With the able help of such ministers as Jiang Shang and Chou Gongdan, the state of Chou had implemented systems favorable to the people and as a result had become more powerful by the day.

Eventually, King Wu saw that the situation was ripe for action. He assembled several tens of thousands of superior troops and set out to attack the capital of the state of Shang. Along the way, his ranks were swelled by various tribes who had also been increasingly dissatisfied with the rule of King Zhou. King Wu reinforced their discontent by pointing out the heinous crimes of the ruler of Shang and mobilized all to rise up and end his reign. The alliance of troops quickly advanced to a place called Muye, not far from the capital of Shang, now in a place

now called Qi County, in Henan Province.

The main force of the Shang armies was already engaged in war at the time, in the east, and was unable to return quickly to defend the capital. King Zhou had no alternative but to force a large contingent of slaves to fight on his behalf, ordering them to Muye to do battle against King Wu. These slaves hardly had enough to eat, however, and certainly had no strength with which to fight for King Zhou. What's more, they hated his dominion over them and so promptly surrendered to King Wu and helped him attack. King Zhou fled to a high tower within the palace from which there was no escape. With his kingdom lost, he had the tower torched and committed suicide, although some people say that in the end he was caught by King Wu and put to death.

The great Shang Dynasty thereby came to an end. King Wu founded the Chou Dynasty (1046–256 BCE), which was to be in existence longer than any other dynasty in Chinese history.

秦始皇统一六国

原文：

yíng qín shì　　shǐ jiān bìng
嬴 秦 氏 ，始 兼 并 。

故事：

　　秦始皇是秦王朝（前221—前206）的开创者，建立了中国第一个统一的封建王朝。他也是中国历史上最有争议的皇帝。不管怎么说，他对中国乃至世界历史都产生了深远的影响。

　　秦始皇所生活的战国末年，经过很长时期的战争，还剩下了七个诸侯国。秦始皇十三岁时继承秦国的王位，二十多岁的时候就实际掌握了大权。他是一个雄心勃勃的人，决心完成此前所有国王都没有做到的一件事，那就是统一其他六国。为此，他首先在秦国推行一些强有力的措施，使秦国强大起来。

　　到他三十岁时，秦国的国力已远远超过其他六国。于是，秦始皇开始发动统一六国的战争。对于这场战争，他有很清楚的设想，就是由近及远，各个击破。但在实际进程

中，他又善于随时调整自己的战略。

首先被秦国灭亡的是实力弱小的韩国，然后就是当时六国中实力最强的赵国。秦始皇利用赵国发生地震和灾荒的机会，派兵进攻赵国，双方相持了一年，秦国使用计谋，使赵王逮捕并处死了赵国的主将李牧等人。秦军趁机加强进攻，终于攻占了赵国的首都。这一来，其他国家就更无力阻挡秦军的强大攻势了，燕（yān）国、魏国、楚国、齐国也先后被灭亡，其中，与南方的强国楚国之间的战争进行得比较激烈。

经过九年的战争，秦始皇终于实现了统一六国的雄心壮志，并着手建立一个统一的大帝国。他决定称自己为"皇帝"，这样，他就成为中国历史上第一个使用"皇帝"称号的帝王。以后，"皇帝"就成为中国最高统治者的称谓。

秦始皇建立了一套中央集权的国家管理机构，这种做法一直为后来的各个王朝所仿效。地方的行政机构，则分为郡、县两级。全国分成三十六郡，以后增加到了四十一郡。

战国时期，各个国家的文字、货币和度量衡制度都不一样，秦始皇发现这样很不方便，而且不利于统一的管理。他派人制定了一套统一的标准，下令全国都要使用相同的文字、度量衡制度和货币。另外，他还命令统一车辆的大小，并根据这个大小修建道路，这样，不论哪个地方造的车子，都可以通行全国。这些措施对中国社会和文化影响深远。

秦始皇统一中国，结束诸侯国长期割据混战的局面，促

进各地区、各民族之间的经济文化交流，这是很了不起的贡
献。但他又是一个实行残暴统治的皇帝，很快激起了人民的
反抗，所以秦朝并没有如他所希望的那样永远存在下去，相
反，短短十多年后就被推翻了。

Qin Shi Huang Di Unifies the Six States

Qin Shi Huang Di was the founder of the Qin Dynasty (221–206 BCE), which is regarded as the first "feudal dynasty" ruling over unified states in China. Qin Shi Huang Di was also the most controversial emperor in Chinese history. Whatever the verdict on this man, he had a profound influence not only on Chinese but on world history.

Qin Shi Huang, as he is typically called, lived in the latter years of the Warring States period. After warfare and consolidation, seven states remained that were known as "Principalities," ruled by princes. Qin Shi Huang was thirteen when he assumed the throne in the state of Qin, and he was twenty when he took over actual ruling power. Endowed with extreme ambition, he was determined to complete the task of uniting the other six states under his control, something no ruler had been able to do. In order to do this, he first implemented forceful measures in the state of Qin that would enable it to become more powerful.

By the time he was thirty years old, the national strength of the state of Qin far surpassed that of the other six states, and he therefore began his war of consolidation. He had a very clear strategy, which was to proceed from the closest to the more distant, destroying enemy forces one by one. Along the way, however, he was prepared to adjust his tactics in accord with actual circumstances.

The first state to be destroyed by Qin was the smallest and weakest of the six states, called Han. The next was the most powerful among the six, the state of Zhao. Capitalizing on a recent earthquake and natural disasters in that state, Qin Shi Huang attacked and the two sides were in combat for a full year. The state of Qin then used a tricky stratagem to capture the King of Zhao, and also to have a key general

named Li Mu put to death. The Qin armies took advantage of the opportunity to press their attack and in the end were able to occupy the Zhao capital. After this, the other states were even less able to resist the increased forces of the Qin army and, one by one, the states of Yan, Wei, Chu, and Qi were destroyed. Among these, the battles against the State of Chu in the south were particularly ferocious.

After nine years of warfare, Qin Shi Huang Di finally realized his intense ambition of unifying the other six states under his command. He then began to establish a unified and powerful empire. He decided to call himself "Huang Di," and thereby became the first ruler to designate himself "Emperor" in China. (Previously, rulers or monarchs had called themselves King, or Ruler, but they had not put the two terms Huang and Di together, to signify ultimate ruler. The ruler of Qin was the first, or "shi," to call himself Huang Di, therefore he was the Qin Shi Huang Di.) From then on, "Huang Di," or Emperor, became the term used for the highest authority in power in China.

Qin Shi Huang Di went on to establish a system of centralized power structures for ruling the country, that were to be the model used by later dynasties. Local administrative organizations were divided into the two levels of "jun" or prefecture, and "xian," or county. The entire country was divided into thirty-six prefectures initially, a number that later was expanded to forty-one.

During the Warring States period, all scripts, currencies, and measures in the land had been different, which was not conducive to unified management. Qin Shi Huang Di dispatched officials to implement unified standards. By fiat, he ordered the entire country to use the same script, as well as the same weights and measures and the same currency. He also ordered that the width of axles be standardized in order to allow carts to run along the same ruts in roads. Carts from any one region could thereby travel along roads of any other region. These unifying measures were to have a profound influence on China's social structures and its culture.

Qin Shi Huang Di's unification of China ended a long period of fragmented political entities and ongoing warfare in the country, and enabled cultural and economic communication among different regions and different kinds of people. This was a major contribution, but at the same time the Emperor's violent and cruel methods quickly generated opposition. Instead of going on forever, as planned, the Qin dynasty lasted a brief fifteen years before it was overturned.

楚汉相争

原文：

chuán èr shì   chǔ hàn zhēng

传 二 世， 楚 汉 争。

故事：

秦朝的残暴统治激起人们的反抗，一时之间，出现了许多造反者，秦迅速被推翻了。但是，在那些反秦的人当中，究竟谁能成为新的统治者呢？当时最有实力的两支军队分别由刘邦和项羽率领，为了争做皇帝，两者之间展开了近四年的战争。项羽自称西楚霸王，而刘邦曾被项羽封为汉王，所以他们之间的这场战争就被称为"楚汉相争"。

起初，刘邦一方的势力不如项羽。但是刘邦很有计谋，他抢先攻占了秦的都城咸阳（在现在的陕西省），将秦朝灭亡，并得到了人民的支持。而项羽这时也率领强大的军队赶到了附近，派人让刘邦去见他。刘邦不得已，只得冒险来到项羽的军营，亲自向项羽赔礼道歉。项羽为了表示宽容大度，没有杀掉刘邦，而且封他为汉王。这个时候，项羽成为

中国的实际统治者，向全国各地发号施令。

　　刘邦表面上接受了项羽的命令，实际上却并不甘心就这样放弃皇帝的位子。不久，趁着项羽去进攻另外一个不听从他命令的人，刘邦公开向项羽宣战，从而拉开了楚汉战争的序幕。

　　战争初期，刘邦的处境很糟糕，几乎一直打败仗，在项羽的军队追赶下，到处逃跑。有好几次，他甚至顾不上带走自己的家人，他的父亲、妻子都曾经落入敌军手中。但他并不放弃，重用具有杰出军事才能的将领韩信、彭越等人，让他们分别到别的地方发展势力，以牵制项羽的兵力。这样一来，项羽就没有办法集中兵力消灭刘邦。刘邦的势力又逐渐发展起来，他与韩信等人相互呼应，反而形成了对项羽的包围。项羽只得与刘邦订立盟约，决定以鸿沟（沟通黄河和淮河的人工运河）为界，分别统治中国的东部和西部。

　　项羽以为事情结束了，便按照约定退兵。而刘邦则在谋臣的建议下，下令全力追击楚军。这次轮到项羽被一路追赶，最后，双方在垓下（在现在的安徽省灵璧县）展开决战，楚军大败，只好退到壁垒后面坚守。在汉军重重包围下，楚军的粮食等供应被切断。韩信又让人在夜里唱起楚军家乡的歌曲，很多楚军听了都产生厌战情绪，纷纷逃亡。项羽突围至乌江(在现在的安徽省和县)，全军覆没，他不愿被俘受辱，于是自杀而死。

　　楚汉之争以刘邦的胜利而结束，刘邦建立起了西汉王朝。

Contest between Chu and Han

The cruel and despotic reign of the Qin Dynasty incurred such opposition from the people at large that the dynasty was swiftly overthrown. Among those who had opposed Qin rule, the question now was to decide who had the ability to serve as the new ruler. The two most powerful armies in the land were under the leadership of Liu Bang and Xiang Yu. Contending for the position of Emperor, these two now began a war that was to last four years. Xiang Yu called himself "the Conqueror from Western Chu," while he called Liu Bang the mere "King of Han." In Chinese history, this war was later to be called the Contest between Chu and Han.

Liu Bang's military strength did not equal that of Xiang Yu, at the beginning. He was a master of stratagem, however, and quickly moved to take over the former Qin capital of Xianyang (in today's Shaanxi Province), where he destroyed the Qin and earned the support of the local people. Xiang Yu soon arrived at a nearby spot with his troops, and dispatched a messenger to request a meeting with Liu Bang. Liu Bang had no alternative but to put himself at risk by travelling into Xiang Yu's camp, where he personally apologized to Xiang Yu for his

actions. The apology was accepted and Xiang Yu magnanimously allowed Liu Bang to go on living and even appointed him as "King of Han." At this point, Xiang Yu became the de facto ruler of China, with the power to issue decrees throughout the land.

Meanwhile, Liu Bang ostensibly bowed to Xiang Yu's orders but in fact had not given up his own plan to become emperor. Not long after, when Xiang Yu was distracted by having to deal with some other unruly subject, Liu Bang openly declared war on him, which officially began to great drama of the war between Chu and Han.

At the outset, Liu Bang was in an unfavorable position and indeed was almost defeated. With Xiang Yu chasing after him, he and his armies fled from one place to another. Many times he was unable even to assure the safety of his family, and his father and wife were both taken hostage by the enemy. Still, he persevered, using outstanding military advisors such as Han Xin and Peng Yue, whom he placed in different directions so as to disperse the forces of Xiang Yu. Xiang Yu was therefore unable to concentrate his forces on an all-out attack that might have destroyed Liu Bang. Meanwhile, Liu Bang's military strength gradually increased and he, Han Xin and others were able to surround Xiang Yu's armies. Xiang Yu was forced to come to an agreement whereby they formed an alliance with each side taking a specified territory. They decided that Honggou would be the boundary

between them, with China now being divided into eastern and western regions. Honggou is the manmade canal that connects the Yellow River with the Huai River.

Xiang Yu believed that the matter was now settled. He withdrew his troops as agreed upon in the agreement. On the advice of a particular minister, Liu Bang now commanded his entire army to stage a massive attack. This time, Xiang Yu was on the run. In the end, the two sides fought a final battle at a place called Gaixia (in today's Lingbi County in Anhui Province), where the Chu forces under Xiang Yu were decimated. Xiang Yu retreated to behind some ramparts, where he and his armies were surrounded. Supply lines for grain and materials were cut off. Han Xin now had people sing the homeland melodies of Chu late at night, which demoralized Chu troops. Thoroughly disgusted with war, many abandoned their posts and fled. Xiang Yu and remaining troops broke through the encirclement and made it to the Wu River (in today's He County in Anhui Province), where his entire army was obliterated. Unwilling to endure the humiliation of being taken prisoner, he took his own life.

Liu Bang's victory concluded the contest between Chu and Han. He then founded the Western Han dynasty and became its first "Huang Di," or Emperor, with the reign name of Han Gaozu.

三分天下

原文：

wèi shū wú　zhēng hàn dǐng
魏蜀吴，争汉鼎，

hào sān guó　qì liǎng jìn
号三国，迄两晋。

故事：

东汉末年，中国爆发了大规模的农民起义，各个地方的军事领袖也趁机扩充自己的势力。经过复杂而激烈的混战，全国出现了许多割据势力。这其中，北方的曹操是一个杰出的军事领袖和政治家，经过几年的征战，基本统一了北方。但他不满足于这样的局面，还想一鼓作气，将南北方重新统一起来。

当时，曹操刚刚取得一系列战争的胜利，拥有几十万军队，战斗力强大。中国南方当时的实际统治者是孙权，他从父亲和哥哥手里继承了这个地区的统治权。曹操派人送了一封信给孙权，要求孙权向他投降，接受他的任命，否则就将率领大军南下进攻。

孙权不想向曹操投降，但又害怕曹军的进攻。这时，另一支军队的领袖刘备逃脱了曹操的追赶，派著名的谋士诸葛亮前来与孙权商量联合抗曹的事情。孙权部下一些人也指出，曹军虽然人数众多，但他们是从北方远道而来，物资供应困难，并且北方人不习惯在水上作战，南方军队可以凭借长江这道天险战胜曹军。于是，孙权下定决心，与刘备联合起来抗曹。他任命周瑜为南方军队的统帅。

公元208年，孙、刘联军在长江上的赤壁（在现在的湖北省）一带与曹军交战。孙、刘联军只有几万人，曹军则有二十多万。但曹操部下大部分是北方士兵，为了使他们适应

战船上的生活，曹操下令将战船用链子连接起来。周瑜等人针对曹军这个弱点，采用火攻，在一些船上装满浸油的干柴草，点着之后开向曹军的船队。结果曹军那些连在一起的战船很快就变成一片火海，连岸边的军营也被烧了。孙、刘联军乘势攻击，曹军大败而逃，伤亡惨重。这场赤壁之战成为中国军事史上以弱胜强的著名战例。

赤壁之战后，曹操只好退守黄河流域一带，不敢再轻易南下。而在战争中获胜的孙权在南方长江中下游一带的势力得到巩固，刘备则乘机占领湖北、湖南的大部分地区，又将他的势力扩展到四川。这样，就初步形成了三分天下的局势。

曹操死后，他的儿子曹丕（pī）逼迫东汉最后一个皇帝退位，建立了自己的国家，国号魏。不久，刘备也在成都称帝，国号汉（后人称为蜀汉）。孙权后来也称帝，国号吴。这样，魏、蜀汉、吴三国鼎立的局面最终形成，中国长期处于割据状态。

三国时期（220—280）人才辈出，发生了很多精彩的故事。历史小说《三国演义》将这些人物和故事传播到了世界各地。直到今天，三国人物和事件仍是文学、艺术和电子游戏等的重要题材。

A Three-Part Division
of "All Under Heaven"

At the end of the Eastern Han, large-scale "peasant revolts," or revolts of farmers against the authorities, broke out in China with each general commanding an army often taking advantage of the situation to expand his own power. After a complex and intense period of warfare, a number of separate authorities with their own power appeared in the country, among which the one in the north was led by an outstanding military strategist and political strategist named Cao Cao. After several years of military campaigns, Cao Cao basically unified the northern part of China. Not yet satisfied, he decided to persevere and finish the job, and unify the entire country, both north and south.

Cao Cao consolidated his rule in the north, after a series of battles in which he led several hundred thousand troops, and his power was great. The de facto ruler of the southern part of China was Sun Quan, who had succeeded his father and his brother in controlling the region. Cao Cao now sent an emissary with a letter for Sun Quan, asking him to surrender and submit to his own rule. Otherwise, he would assemble his forces and march south.

Sun Quan did not want to surrender to Cao Cao, but at the same

time he feared the attack. Just at this time another military leader named Liu Bei escaped from Cao Cao's pursuit. Liu Bei sent the famous strategist Zhuge Liang to advise Sun Quan that he would like to join with him in resisting the invasion of Cao Cao. Some among Sun Quan's advisors also pointed out that although Cao Cao had greater forces, he had come from far in the north. Their supply lines were stretched and they were unaccustomed to fighting on water. They felt the southern armies should be able to defeat Cao Cao by using the natural boundary of the Yang-tse River. Sun Quan therefore resolved to fight. He joined forces with Liu Bei. He ordered Zhou Yu to be the commander-in-chief of his southern forces.

In the year 208, the armies of Sun and Liu joined in battle against Cao Cao at a place called Chi Bi, on the Yang-tse River (in today's Hubei Province). The combined forces under Sun and Liu totaled only several tens of thousands of men, while Cao Cao commanded a force of more than 200,000. Cao Cao's armies were mostly northern soldiers, however. In order to acclimate them to life on board ships, Cao Cao ordered that the warships with which they were going to cross the Yang-tse be linked together with chains to stabilize them. Aiming directly at this weakness, Zhou Yu and others used the strategem of "fire attack." They filled ships with oil-soaked pieces of wood, ignited the wood and pointed the ships in the direction of Cao Cao's fleet. Cao

Cao's linked boats were soon in a "sea of fire," while his army camp

on the other shore was also soon incinerated. Sun and Liu pressed the

attack and, suffering severe losses, Cao's army was utterly routed. This

battle of Chi Bi went down in history as a famous military example of

how to conquer strength with weakness.

After the battle of Chi Bi, Cao Cao had little choice but to stay

in the region of the Yellow River in the north, and to leave the south alone. Meanwhile, Sun Quan was able to consolidate his hold on the south. Liu Bei took advantage of the situation to conquer and occupy the region of Hubei and Hunan and also expanded his reach westward into Sichuan. The balance of power created a three-part division of "all under heaven" which was to last for a long time.

After Cao Cao died, his son Cao Pi forced the last emperor of the Eastern Han to abdicate, whereupon Cao Pi established his own political entity, called Wei. Shortly after, Liu Bei also declared himself emperor in Chengdu, and gave his country the name of Han (it was later to be called Shu Han, the word Shu indicating the region around Sichuan). Sun Quan then declared himself emperor as well, and he named his country Wu. Three countries then formed a triangular relationship of Wei, Shu Han, and Wu, a political division that was to become known as the period of the Three Kingdoms.

A number of talented people came to the fore in the Three Kingdoms period (220–280), and the era was rich in marvelous legends and tales. The historical novel called *Romance of the Three Kingdoms* is based on these tales. Characters and events from the Three Kingdoms feature in modern drama and literature to this day, most notably in contemporary television series.

隋炀帝亡国

原文：

dài zhì suí yì tǔ yǔ
迨 至 隋 ， 一 土 宇 。

bú zài chuán shī tǒng xù
不 再 传 ， 失 统 绪 。

故事：

　　隋朝（581—618）的开国皇帝隋文帝结束了南北朝时期中国长期分裂的局面，使中国再次进入和平、强盛的时代。文帝死后，他的儿子杨广登上了皇位，就是中国历史上有名的暴君隋炀帝。

　　其实隋炀帝即位之初，还是很有一番作为的。他开拓了国家的疆土，实行了很多有利于国家发展的制度。为了巩固对全国的统治，方便南方和北方之间的交通运输，隋炀帝决定开凿一条贯通南北的大运河。为此，国家每年都要征发民工上百万人，经过五六年的努力，终于修成了这条全长四千多里（相当于两千多公里）的大运河。这条世界历史上最长

　　的人工运河，对中国社会、经济的发展具有重要意义。

　　大运河开通之后，隋炀帝决定到江南去巡游。他下令造了许多大船，他和皇后所坐的大龙舟有四层高，分隔成几百间装饰华丽的宫室。跟随他出行的官员、宫女和士兵有二十万人，他们分乘几千条大船，浩浩荡荡地走在运河上，头尾相连有二百里长！最后，隋炀帝在江南最繁华的城市扬

州停留下来。

开凿大运河虽然意义深远，但对当时的人民来说，这个艰巨的工程是一场大灾难，在军队的残暴监督下，成千上万的民工惨死在运河工地上。修造数量庞大的船只和满足隋炀帝一行几十万人的吃喝玩乐等需要，也耗费了无数的人力和物力。船队每到一个地方，当地人民就要负责提供吃的喝的，结果很多人家被弄得倾家荡产。更令人民感到绝望的是，炀帝这样走了一次还不够，后来又两次到江南的扬州等地去巡游，每次都使人民蒙受巨大灾难。

在隋炀帝统治时期，他还不断向外扩张，发动了多次战争，但这些军事行动有的遭到彻底失败。不论胜败，连年的征战都使隋的人口和财富迅速消失，社会生产遭到严重破坏。而为了支付战争、巡游和自己享乐的费用，隋炀帝不断加重人民的劳役和赋税。

人民被压迫得无法生存，各地纷纷爆发了反对隋炀帝的起义。最后，隋炀帝的部下在扬州发动兵变，勒死了这个残暴的统治者。虽然官员们又立了一个年幼的皇帝，但几年之后，隋朝还是灭亡了，取而代之的是唐朝。

Sui Yangdi Loses His Country

The founder of the Sui dynasty (581–618), Sui Wendi, succeeded in ending the long period of divided political power in China that was known as the Northern and Southern Dynasties. He led the country into a peaceful and prosperous age. After his death, his son Yang Guang ascended the throne, the man who later became infamous as the cruel tyrant Sui Yangdi.

Sui Yangdi was successful in a number of ways at the beginning of his rule. He opened up China's frontiers, "developing the wastelands," and he instituted a number of systems that were beneficial to economic growth. In order to consolidate his power over the entire country as well as to make transportation and communication more convenient between north and south, Sui Yangdi made the decision to build what is known as the Great Canal. To build this canal, the government requisitioned more than one million laborers from among the people every year. The work took between five and six years, and eventually resulted in a canal of more than 4 000 li, which is equivalent to over 2000 kilometers. Built in the 7th Century, this remains the longest man-made canal in human history and it has had a profound impact on

Chinese social and economic development.

After the canal was finished, Sui Yangdi decided to take a journey "south of the river" to make an inspection. He ordered the construction of a number of large ships. The one in which he and his empress travelled was a huge "dragon boat," four stories high, divided into several hundred palace chambers that were all ornately furnished. Some 200,000 officials, palace women and soldiers accompanied Sui Yang Di on the trip. Arrayed in several thousand boats, the entire procession made its stately way down the Canal—from front to back, the entourage was said to have measured two hundred li. At the end of the canal, Sui Yangdi stopped to rest a while at Yangzhou, the most prosperous city south of the river at the time.

Although the building of the Canal had great significance for the country, for the common people it was a major calamity. Under cruel overseers, many thousands of workers died in the course of its construction. When Sui Yangdi's procession passed by, local people had to supply the daily provisions for several tens of thousands of people. Families were bankrupted in the process. What was worse, the emperor made the journey not once, but two more times, each time travelling all the way to Yangzhou and bringing calamity to the common people.

During his rule, Sui Yangdi ceaselessly expanded the borders of China, mobilizing a number of wars although some of these cam-

paigns met with total defeat. Whether victorious or unsuccessful, the result of the campaigns was an inevitable decline in the population of the country and in its treasury as the economy was disrupted. In order to support his wars as well as his expeditions and the expense of his own extravagances, Sui Yangdi continuously levied higher taxes and higher requirements for conscripted labor.

Pressed beyond endurance, people in a number of places began to rise in revolt. In the end, Sui Yangdi's own troops in Yangzhou staged a mutiny and forcefully killed this despotic ruler. Although officials quickly installed a young ruler on the throne, the Sui dynasty came to an end a few years later and was succeeded by the Tang dynasty.

宋太祖黄袍加身

原文：

yán sòng xīng　　shòu zhōu shàn
炎宋兴，受周禅，

shí bā chuán　　nán běi hùn
十八传，南北混。

故事：

五代的最后一个朝代是后周（951—960）。后周的皇帝周世宗死后，他七岁的儿子继承了皇位。新皇帝年纪太小，由宰相们帮助他处理政事。这时候，大将赵匡胤（yìn）看到夺取政权的时机和条件已经成熟，经过精心策划，发动了历史上有名的"陈桥兵变"。

事情发生在新皇帝即位之后的第一个新年，忽然北方边境传来警报，说强大的敌国将要入侵。正在举行新年庆典的小皇帝和大臣们都很惊慌，两位宰相提议，让赵匡胤统率军队去抵抗。赵匡胤本来就掌握着全国最精锐的部队，这次把其他军队的指挥权也交给了他。

赵匡胤率领大军出发，他弟弟赵匡义、他最信任的谋士赵普和其他一些忠于他的将军都跟在他身边。走到离都城开封（在现在的河南）不远的陈桥驿，他命令军队停下来驻扎。到了晚上，忠于赵匡胤的将军们宣传说："皇帝年龄这么小，我们拼死打败了敌人，又有谁知道我们的功劳呢？不如先立赵将军为天子，然后再去打仗。"他们找到赵匡义和赵普，声称愿意拥戴赵匡胤为皇帝。赵匡义和赵普就带着这些人赶来见赵匡胤。

发生这件大事的时候，赵匡胤在做什么呢？据说他当时因为喝醉了酒而在睡觉。赵匡义、赵普先进营帐去向他说明这件事，没等说完，那些全副武装的将军们就迫不及待地闯

进来，把一件表示皇帝身份的黄袍披在赵匡胤的身上。众人跪在地上向他行礼，称他为"万岁"，簇拥着他来到军中。

赵匡胤对众人说："你们拥护我当皇帝，那么你们愿意听从我的命令吗？"大家都高喊愿意，于是赵匡胤下达了一系列指令，要求不随便动用武力，不侵犯小皇帝母子和朝廷大臣，不抢国库。将军们都答应了。于是，这支军队又跟着赵匡胤回到开封，守城的将军们也赞成赵匡胤做皇帝。

他们一起去见宰相，说明这件事。赵匡胤装出为难的样子说："将士们逼着我做皇帝，你们说怎么办？"面对明晃晃的刀枪，宰相们吓得不敢说什么，只能去劝小皇帝把皇位让给赵匡胤。

就这样，赵匡胤通过一场基本没有流血的兵变，取得了皇位，建立北宋，结束了混乱的五代时期。赵匡胤就是宋太祖，北宋的都城仍然定在开封。

Song Taizu Is "Draped in the Imperial Yellow Robes by His Supporters"

The last dynasty in the Five Dynasties period was Latter Zhou (951 –960). After the Emperor of this dynasty died, his seven-year-old son succeeded to the throne. Since the new Emperor was too young to rule, several ministers assisted him in managing affairs. A powerful general named Zhao Kuangyin looked over this situation and recognized that the time and conditions were ripe for seizing power. He planned his strategy in minute detail, and the results went down in history as the famous "Mutiny of Chen Bridge."

The event occurred in the year in which the young emperor assumed the throne. Alarming news suddenly issued from the northern borders that seemed to indicate that a huge enemy was preparing to invade. The little emperor, just in the process of performing the New Year's rites, and his senior ministers were in a panic. Two Prime Ministers then recommended that General Zhao Kuangyin be placed at the head of an army to fight back. Zhao Kuangyin was already in command of the finest troops in the country. All other troops were now put under him as well.

Zhao Kuangyin then led his massive army out on the march, to-

gether with his little brother Zhao Kuangyi, his most trusted strategist Zhao Pu, and several generals who were loyal to him. Not far from the capital city of Kaifeng (in today's Henan Province), they stopped at a place called the Chen Bridge Post, a wayside stop for putting up horses. He ordered his troops to make camp in the vicinity. Around evening time, the loyal generals began to propagandize among the troops. They said, "You know, the little emperor is very young. Here we are risking our lives to defeat the enemy but who is going to know about it or recognize all our hard work? It might be best to make Zhao Kuangyin Son of Heaven first, and then after that we can go fight this war." The generals searched out Zhao Kuangyi, the little brother, and Zhao Pu, the strategist, who were both in agreement and supported making Zhao Kuangyin emperor. The brother and the strategist then led the way to have a meeting with Zhao Kuangyin to ask him about it.

While all this was going on, it is said that Zhao Kuangyin was actually sound asleep, since he had drunk too much. Entering his tent, Zhao Kuangyi and Zhao Pu explained the matter to him. Before they had even finished, generals waiting outside, who were bristling with weapons, rushed in and presented him with a yellow robe. This they draped over his body. They then kneeled down in front of him and performed ceremonial rites, declaring him to be "wan sui" or long-lived, and supporting him as they took him out among the troops.

At that point, Zhao Kuangyin declared to all those around him, "If you want me to be emperor, are you willing to follow my orders?" Everyone shouted loudly that they were. Zhao Kuangyin then proceeded to issue a series of orders. He required that soldiers were not allowed to use weapons willy nilly, that they were not allowed to harm the young emperor or his mother or any of the senior officials at the court, and that they were not allowed to pillage the State treasury. The generals all promptly agreed to these things. The army then followed behind the Zhao Kuangyin as they marched into Kaifeng, where generals guarding the city promptly agreed to support him as emperor.

Together, they went in to meet with senior Ministers to the emperor, to report on this event. Zhao Kuangyin pretended to be forced into the position. "The Generals are forcing me to be Emperor," he said, "What can I do?" Faced with the gleaming weapons on all those around them, the Ministers were speechless with fear and advised the Little Emperor to hand over his throne.

This is how Zhao Kuangyin accomplished the feat of being made emperor of China without having to spill a drop of blood. He then established the dynasty called the Northern Song, which brought the chaos of the Five Dynasties period to an end. Zhao Kuangyin was to become famous in Chinese history as the legendary Song Taizu, and the capital of the Northern Song continued to be Kaifeng.

《三字经》

rén zhī chū　　xìng běn shàn　　xìng xiāng jìn　　xí xiāngyuǎn
人之初，性本善。性相近，习相远。

gǒu bù jiào　　xìng nǎi qiān　　jiào zhī dào　　guì yǐ zhuān
苟不教，性乃迁。教之道，贵以专。

xī mèng mǔ　　zé lín chǔ　　zǐ bù xué　　duàn jī zhù
昔孟母，择邻处，子不学，断机杼。

dòu yān shān　　yǒu yì fāng　　jiào wǔ zǐ　　míng jù yáng
窦燕山，有义方，教五子，名俱扬。

yǎng bù jiào　　fù zhī guò　　jiào bù yán　　shī zhī duò
养不教，父之过。教不严，师之惰。

zǐ bù xué　　fēi suǒ yí　　yòu bù xué　　lǎo hé wéi
子不学，非所宜。幼不学，老何为？

yù bù zhuó　　bù chéng qì　　rén bù xué　　bù zhī yì
玉不琢，不成器。人不学，不知义。

wéi rén zǐ　　fāng shào shí　　qīn shī yǒu　　xí lǐ yí
为人子，方少时，亲师友，习礼仪。

xiāng jiǔ líng　　néng wēn xí　　xiào yú qīn　　suǒ dāng zhí
香九龄，能温席，孝于亲，所当执。

róng sì suì　　néng ràng lí　　tì yú zhǎng　　yí xiān zhī
融四岁，能让梨，弟于长，宜先知。

shǒu xiào tì　　cì jiàn wén　　zhī mǒu shù　　shì mǒu wén
首孝弟，次见闻，知某数，识某文。

yī ér shí　　shí ér bǎi　　bǎi ér qiān　　qiān ér wàn
一而十，十而百，百而千，千而万。

sān cái zhě　　tiān dì rén　　sān guāng zhě　　rì yuè xīng
三才者，天地人。三光者，日月星。

sān gāng zhě　　jūn chén yì　　fù zǐ qīn　　fū fù shùn
三纲者，君臣义，父子亲，夫妇顺。

yuē chūn xià　　yuē qiū dōng　　cǐ sì shí　　yùn bù qióng
日春夏，日秋冬，此四时，运不穷。

yuē nán běi　yuē xī dōng　cǐ sì fāng　yìng hū zhōng
曰南北，曰西东，此四方，应乎中。

yuē shuǐ huǒ　mù jīn tǔ　cǐ wǔ xíng　běn hū shù
曰水火，木金土，此五行，本乎数。

yuē rén yì　lǐ zhì xìn　cǐ wǔ cháng　bù róng wěn
曰仁义，礼智信，此五常，不容紊。

dào liáng shū　mài shǔ jì　cǐ liù gǔ　rén suǒ shí
稻粱菽，麦黍稷，此六谷，人所食。

mǎ niú yáng　jī quǎn shǐ　cǐ liù chù　rén suǒ sì
马牛羊，鸡犬豕，此六畜，人所饲。

yuē xǐ nù　yuē āi jù　ài wù yù　qī qíng jù
曰喜怒，曰哀惧，爱恶欲，七情具。

páo tǔ gé　mù shí jīn　sī yǔ zhú　nǎi bā yīn
匏土革，木石金，丝与竹，乃八音。

gāo zēng zǔ　fù ér shēn　shēn ér zǐ　zǐ ér sūn
高曾祖，父而身，身而子，子而孙。

zì zǐ sūn　zhì xuán zēng　nǎi jiǔ zú　rén zhī lún
自子孙，至玄曾，乃九族，人之伦。

父子恩，夫妇从，兄则友，弟则恭，

长幼序，友与朋，君则敬，臣则忠，

此十义，人所同。

凡训蒙，须讲究。详训诂，明句读。

为学者，必有初。小学终，至四书。

论语者，二十篇，群弟子，记善言。

孟子者，七篇止，讲道德，说仁义。

作中庸，子思笔，中不偏，庸不易。

作大学，乃曾子，自修齐，至平治。

孝经通，四书熟，如六经，始可读。

诗书易，礼春秋，号六经，当讲求。

有连山，有归藏，有周易，三易详。

有典谟，有训诰，有誓命，书之奥。

我周公，作周礼。著六官，存治体。

大小戴，注礼记，述圣言，礼乐备。

曰国风，曰雅颂，号四诗，当讽咏。

诗既亡，春秋作，寓褒贬，别善恶。

三传者，有公羊，有左氏，有谷梁。

jīng jì míng，fāng dú zǐ，cuō qí yào，jì qí shì
经既明，方读子，撮其要，记其事。

wǔ zǐ zhě，yǒu xún yáng，wén zhōng zǐ，jí lǎo zhuāng
五子者，有荀扬，文中子，及老庄。

jīng zǐ tōng，dú zhū shǐ。kǎo shì xì，zhī zhōng shǐ
经子通，读诸史。考世系，知终始。

zì xī nóng，zhì huáng dì，hào sān huáng，jū shàng shì
自羲农，至黄帝，号三皇，居上世。

táng yǒu yú，hào èr dì，xiāng yī xùn，chēng shèng shì
唐有虞，号二帝，相揖逊，称盛世。

xià yǒu yǔ，shāng yǒu tāng，zhōu wén wǔ，chēng sān wáng
夏有禹，商有汤，周文武，称三王。

xià chuán zǐ，jiā tiān xià，sì bǎi zǎi，qiān xià shè
夏传子，家天下，四百载，迁夏社。

tāng fà xià，guó hào shāng，liú bǎi zǎi，zhì zhòu wáng
汤伐夏，国号商，六百载，至纣亡。

zhōu wǔ wáng，shǐ zhū zhòu，bā bǎi zǎi，zuì cháng jiǔ
周武王，始诛纣，八百载，最长久。

zhōu zhé dōng　wáng gāng zhuì　chěng gān gē　shàng yóu shuì
周辙东，王纲坠，逞干戈，尚游说。

shǐ chūn qiū　zhōng zhàn guó　wǔ bà qiáng　qī xióng chū
始春秋，终战国，五霸强，七雄出。

yíng qín shì　shǐ jiān bìng　chuán èr shì　chǔ hàn zhēng
嬴秦氏，始兼并，传二世，楚汉争。

gāo zǔ xīng　hàn yè jiàn　zhì xiào píng　wáng mǎng cuàn
高祖兴，汉业建，至孝平，王莽篡。

guāng wǔ xīng　wéi dōng hàn　sì bǎi nián　zhōng yú xiàn
光武兴，为东汉，四百年，终于献。

wèi shǔ wú　zhèng hàn dǐng　hào sān guó　qì liǎng jìn
魏蜀吴，争汉鼎，号三国，迄两晋。

sòng qí jì　liáng chén chéng　wéi nán cháo　dū jīn líng
宋齐继，梁陈承，为南朝，都金陵。

běi yuán wèi　fēn dōng xī　yǔ wén zhōu　yǔ gāo qí
北元魏，分东西，宇文周，与高齐。

dài zhì suí　yì tǔ yǔ　bú zài chuán　shī tǒng xù
迨至隋，一土宇，不再传，失统绪。

táng gāo zǔ　　qǐ yì shī　　chú suí luàn　　chuàng guó jī

唐高祖，起义师，除隋乱，创国基。

èr shí chuán　　sān bǎi zǎi　　liáng miè zhī　　guó nǎi gǎi

二十传，三百载，梁灭之，国乃改。

liáng táng jìn　　jí hàn zhōu　　chēng wǔ dài　　jiē yǒu yóu

梁唐晋，及汉周，称五代，皆有由。

yán sòng xīng　　shòu zhōu shàn　　shí bā chuán　　nán běi hùn

炎宋兴，受周禅，十八传，南北混。

liáo yǔ jīn　　dì hào fēn　　dài miè liáo　　sòng yóu cún

辽与金，帝号纷，迨灭辽，宋犹存。

zhì yuán xīng　　jīn xù xiē　　yǒu sòng shì　　yì tóng miè

至元兴，金绪歇，有宋世，一同灭，

bìng zhōng guó　　jiān róng dí

并中国，兼戎狄。

míng tài zǔ　　jiǔ qīn shī　　chuán jiàn wén　　fāng sì sì

明太祖，久亲师，传建文，方四祀，

qiān běi jīng　　yǒng lè sì　　dài chóng zhēn　　méi shān shì

迁北京，永乐嗣，迨崇祯，煤山逝。

qīng tài zǔ　　yīng jǐng mìng　　jìng sì fāng　　kè dà dìng
清太祖，膺景命，靖四方，克大定。

zhì xuān tǒng　　nǎi dà tóng　　shí èr shì　　qīng zuò zhōng
至宣统，乃大同，十二世，清祚终。

dú shǐ zhě　　kǎo shí lù　　tōng gǔ jīn　　ruò qīn mù
读史者，考实录，通古今，若亲目。

kǒu ér sòng　　xīn ér wéi　　zhāo yú sī　　xī yú sī
口而诵，心而惟，朝于斯，夕于斯。

xī zhòng ní　　shī xiàng tuó　　gǔ shèng xián　　shàng qín xué
昔仲尼，师项橐，古圣贤，尚勤学。

zhào zhōng lìng　　dú lǔ lún　　bǐ jì shì　　xué qiě qín
赵中令，读鲁论，彼既仕，学且勤。

pī pú biān　　xiāo zhū jiǎn　　bǐ wú shū　　qiě zhī miǎn
披蒲编，削竹简，彼无书，且知勉。

tóu xuán liáng　　zhuī cì gǔ　　bǐ bù jiāo　　zì qín kǔ
头悬梁，锥刺股，彼不教，自勤苦。

rú náng yíng　　rú yìng xuě　　jiā suī pín　　xué bú chuò
如囊萤，如映雪，家虽贫，学不辍。

rú fù xīn　rú guà jiǎo　shēn suī láo　yóu kǔ zhuó
如负薪，如挂角，身虽劳，犹苦卓。

sù lǎo quán　èr shí qī　shǐ fā fèn　dú shū jǐ
苏老泉，二十七，始发愤，读书籍。

bǐ jì lǎo　yóu huǐ chí　ěr xiǎo shēng　yí zǎo sī
彼既老，犹悔迟；尔小生，宜早思。

ruò liáng hào　bā shí èr　duì dà tíng　kuí duō shì
若梁灏，八十二，对大廷，魁多士。

bǐ jì chéng　zhòng chēng yì　ěr xiǎo shēng　yí lì zhì
彼既成，众称异；尔小生，宜立志。

yíng bā suì　néng yǒng shī　mì qī suì　néng fù qí
莹八岁，能咏诗；泌七岁，能赋棋。

bǐ yǐng wù　rén chēng qí　ěr yòu xué　dāng xiào zhī
彼颖悟，人称奇；尔幼学，当效之。

cài wén jī　néng biàn qín　xiè dào yùn　néng yǒng yín
蔡文姬，能辨琴；谢道韫，能咏吟。

bǐ nǚ zǐ　qiě cōng mǐn　ěr nán zǐ　dāng zì jǐng
彼女子，且聪敏；尔男子，当自警。

táng liù yàn　fāng qī suì　jǔ shén tóng　zuò zhèng zì
唐刘晏，方七岁，举神童，作正字。

bǐ suī yòu　shēn yǐ shì　ěr yòu xué　miǎn ér zhì
彼虽幼，身已仕；尔幼学，勉而致。

yǒu wéi zhě　yì ruò shì
有为者，亦若是。

quǎn shǒu yè　jī sī chén　gǒu bù xué　hé wéi rén
犬守夜，鸡司晨，苟不学，曷为人？

cán tǔ sī　fēng niàng mì　rén bù xué　bù rú wù
蚕吐丝，蜂酿蜜，人不学，不如物。

yòu ér xué　zhuàng ér xíng　shàng zhì jūn　xià zé mín
幼而学，壮而行，上致君，下泽民。

yáng míng shēng　xiǎn fù mǔ　guāng yú qián　yù yú hòu
扬名声，显父母，光于前，裕于后。

rén yí zǐ　jīn mǎn yíng　wǒ jiào zǐ　wéi yì jīng
人遗子，金满籯；我教子，惟一经。

qín yǒu gōng　xì wú yì　jiè zhī zāi　yí miǎn lì
勤有功，戏无益，戒之哉，宜勉力。

图书在版编目（CIP）数据

《三字经》故事：汉英对照/郁辉著；（美）艾梅
霞(Avery,M.)译.—北京：五洲传播出版社，2009.12
（中国蒙学经典故事丛书）
ISBN 978-7-5085-1738-4

Ⅰ.①三…　Ⅱ.①郁…②艾…　Ⅲ.①汉语–对外汉
语教学–语言读物 ②汉语–古代–启蒙读物
Ⅳ.①H195.5②H194.1

中国版本图书馆CIP数据核字（2009）第207511号

主　　　编：荆孝敏　邓锦辉
副 主 编：王　峰
顾　　　问：赵启正　沈锡麟　潘　岳
　　　　　　周黎明（美）　李莎（加）　威廉·林赛（英）
监　　　制：林武汉
著　　　者：郁　辉
翻　　　译：艾梅霞（美）
责 任 编 辑：王　峰
设 计 指 导：缪　惟
设 计 制 作：潘宏伟　林国霞
插　　　图：刘向伟　刘　倩

《三字经》故事

出版发行：五洲传播出版社
社　　　址：北京市海淀区莲花池东路北小马厂6号华天大厦
邮政编码：100038
电　　　话：010-58891281
传　　　真：010-58891281
制版单位：北京锦绣圣艺文化发展有限公司
印　　　刷：北京彩和坊印刷有限公司
开　　　本：787x1092　1/16
印　　　张：12.75
版　　　次：2010年1月第1版　2010年1月第1次印刷
书　　　号：ISBN 978-7-5085-1738-4
定　　　价：79.00元